BETA
UNTAMED

Feral Pack: Book Two

EVE LANGLAIS

PROLOGUE

BEFORE ASHER STARTED WORKING AT THE RANCH...

The cowards jumped Asher as he left work.

As a bartender in downtown Edmonton, he was always the last one to leave because he made sure all the girls on staff got into their cars and on their way safely before he locked up. Which left him alone in the alley when the gang ambushed him.

Tired after his ten-hour shift, he never heard or smelled them coming. Blame the clanking of the HVAC system and the stench of the dumpsters.

As he walked past the garbage bin, headed for his motorcycle, a fist clocked him out of nowhere and his head snapped back. Before he could recover, the pummeling came fast and furious. Boots to his ribs. Blows to his face.

Things cracked.

Bruised.

Bled.

And fucking hurt until he passed out and woke in the hospital. Or so he assumed by the smell of antiseptic and the steady pinging of machines. The swelling around his eyes meant he could barely open them. Via a tiny slit, he noted an IV in his arm dripped fluids.

"Asher!" The cry drew his squinting attention to the left side of his bed, where his sister stood, expression drawn, hands wringing in anxiety.

"Hey, Winnie." Asher tried to smile for her, only to grimace instead as his bruised jaw protested.

"Thank goodness you're awake. I'll get the nurse."

"No, nurse. Just you. Please." He wasn't ready to deal with anyone else yet.

Tears filled her eyes. "Oh, Asher." Not the first time she'd cried over him. His pretty face and loose tongue meant he drew more than his fair share of fights. He also liked doing the dumb shit brash young men enjoyed like jumping off cliffs into water without checking the level or rocks first. He'd spent part of that summer in a cast.

He tried to push himself up and grimaced as pain shot through him.

At his expression, she hastened to jab at a button,

angling the bed so he could sit at an incline. He should have remained lying down, not that he mentioned the discomfort to his baby sister.

"I'm okay, Winnie. Betcha it looks worse than I feel." A lie. He felt plenty shitty.

Her lower lip wobbled. "Do you know who attacked you? The police couldn't find any clues."

"No idea. It was dark. Guess it was my turn for a mugging." Another fib. He'd gotten a glimpse of the ringleader. Rocco Durante. Son of the Pack's Alpha. A veritable asshole and a bully when paired with his two closest allies, Larry and Ben.

"I was so worried. The hospital said you showed signs of a brain bleed. They weren't sure you'd wake up or be okay."

He wouldn't have survived if he were human. A Were had a better constitution than most. "Bah. It will take more than a few love taps to hurt me," he soothed. He hated seeing Winnie, the baby sister he'd always coddled, worried. "Surprised Mom isn't here." Ever since his dad died, more than ten years now, Mom had a tendency to hover.

"She just left. She's been at the hospital since they brought you in."

"How long?" He felt stiff, and not all of it was because of his wounds. His muscles protested his long nap.

"Someone found you yesterday morning, and it's late afternoon now."

A wince tugged his mouth. He must have been in really bad shape to be unconscious that long. No wonder they thought he might not recover.

Winnie kept talking. "Mom is going to be so peeved you woke up while she went to grab a shower and something to eat."

"Food sounds good about now." His body would require plenty of nutrition to speed up the healing process.

Winnie's expression brightened. "You're hungry? I'll let your nurse know to bring you a tray. You should also be checked over."

"No nurse. They'll want to feed me shitty hospital food." He'd had it before. Bland broth. Stale bread. A carton of milk. "I want real stuff. I'm a growing boy." He wasn't sure his winsome smile had the proper effect given Winnie swallowed hard and blinked back fat tears.

Her words were choked as she muttered, "I'll run to the coffee shop across the street and grab you something."

Before he could tell her not to leave, she was gone. She obviously said something to a nurse because one wearing a patterned scrub top with matching cap came bustling in.

"Look who's back in the land of the living." Her greeting was boisterous. "How are you feeling?"

He wanted to snarl that he'd rather be dead, or at least still unconscious, because he hurt all over. But that wasn't the Asher he showed to the world. He managed a wan smile that didn't send the nurse screaming and said, "Not great, but I'll live. Thanks for looking after me."

"Bah, it was no problem. You were pretty quiet." The nurse offered a smile as she placed her fingers on his wrist, eyeing her watch.

They exchanged small talk, the bantering kind to soften her toward him. Asher had a way of putting people, especially women, at ease. Sometimes more a curse than a boon.

As Nurse Marge, according to her nametag, checked him over and took his vitals, detailing how lucky he was to be alive, he kept his replies vague. Chances were he'd have to chat with the police, and he didn't want to screw up whatever story he settled on. Despite knowing who put him in the hospital, he couldn't exactly tattle. One didn't rat on other Pack members. Besides, Rocco—the man leading the beating—had reason to be angry with Asher.

As Marge finished checking his vitals, a sound at the door caught his attention.

A beautiful woman stood framed. Melinda.

Rocco's ex-fiancée and the reason for his current condition.

Marge eyed Melinda with a frown. "Are you family?"

"A friend," Melinda declared, suddenly flustered.

"FAMILY ONLY." Marge moved in Melinda's direction to escort her out.

"Please, Marge, I'd appreciate it ever so much if you'd let my girlfriend stay." Asher uttered the plea using his best poor-little-boy expression and voice. It worked even with his face battered.

Marge wagged a finger. "Only for a few minutes. The doctor will be in to see you momentarily."

"You're an angel," he declared.

Melinda said nothing until the nurse left, and then it emerged in a soft rush. "I'm sorry, Asher. I never expected this to happen."

"I kind of expected it. Can't really blame Rocco either. Losing you would be a hard pill for him to swallow." Melinda had, until recently, been engaged to Rocco, but then she met Asher and it was love at first sight.

Poor Rocco. He must have been devastated when she broke things off. Pity he'd found out about

Melinda and Asher so quick. They'd been so discreet last weekend, their first time together. A torrid moment he'd never forget.

He'd not seen Melinda since the kiss he'd given her before she got in her car and drove back to the city. As for him, he'd enjoyed a leisurely meal at a local restaurant then took the scenic route so he'd arrive much later. It wouldn't do to rub their new couple status in Rocco's face. They could wait a while before going out in public.

Asher had texted Melinda when he arrived home, missing her already. She didn't reply, but Sundays she usually had dinner with her family. He'd tried again the next day before work. Oddly, she'd still not replied.

But she was here now. His mate, whom he couldn't smell because of his swollen nose. He had no doubt, though, that after the passion they'd experienced, she bore his scent. The distinct aroma a sign of a true claiming, a rare bond that occurred when two fated people had orgasmic sex for the first time.

He reached for her hand, but she didn't grab it. Instead, she remained standing with her hands tightly clasped.

"Are you okay?" he asked since she appeared upset. "I know I'm a little hideous right now, but I'll heal. Promise."

"I'm sure you will." She glanced over her shoulder.

So beautiful. From the first time he'd seen Melinda, his blood boiled. They'd barely known each other or spoken much before they got together. What was there to say? He knew how he felt, and she had to feel it, too, given what she'd given up to be with him.

"I'm glad you're here," he said, reaching for her again. "Come closer. I won't bite." As if he'd ever leave a mark on her smooth skin.

Once more, she remained in her spot. "We need to talk. About Rocco."

He stiffened. "What about Rocco? Did he threaten you? I'll kill him if he did."

"No. He would never lay a hand on me."

"Then what is it?"

"I didn't actually dump him," she blurted out before biting her lower lip.

"What?" He must have heard her wrong. "You told me you had." He had insisted she be free before he'd get involved. A hard thing to tell a woman who tempted his moral fiber by saying, "*I can't stop thinking about you.*"

"You didn't seriously think I'd cancel my engagement? The wedding is two weeks away."

"I'm confused." Actually, he wasn't. He'd heard

her quite clearly, and what he understood peeved. "Are you saying you never planned to ditch Rocco?"

She nodded.

"You said you wanted me. Why the fuck did you lie to me?" The expletive slipped out.

"I didn't lie about wanting you. Just the part when I told you I'd dump Rocco."

"Why?"

"Because you left me no choice."

He blinked. "The choice was if you want to be with me, you have to be single. But instead, you chose to tell a bald-faced lie just so I'd make you cream." A crude thing to state. The throbbing pain in his body made it hard to feel charitable.

"I know it was selfish. I just couldn't help myself. I wanted you so bad."

The words managed to reassure him that his cock remained functional. He'd wanted her badly, too, else he would have never even considered dating another guy's girl.

Could he really blame her? As his mate, she couldn't deny the connection between them. While he wished she'd done things in the proper order, at least now the wolf was out of the trap.

"Well, I won't say I'm happy about how things transpired, but at least now Rocco knows and we can be together."

She shook her head. "I'm sorry, Asher. You're a super guy, sexy and awesome in bed, but we can't be together."

"I don't understand." Her words made no sense. Or was it the pounding in his head making comprehension elusive? "You said you loved me." Yelled it as he pounded into her as a matter of fact.

"Yeah, but—"

"There is no but. Either you love me or you don't. There is no middle ground." A harsh rebuke. He'd never used such a stern tone with her before.

"Fine then. I don't."

The claim hit him in the gut. "What's happening?" Had his beating addled his wits? Was this some kind of coma nightmare?

Her expression turned haughty. "What's happening is you're acting dense. Did you really think I'd dump Rocco, the Alpha's son who is going to inherit leadership of the Pack one day, for a bartender?"

The sneer turned her into someone he didn't recognize. The beauty that had captivated him was apparently only on the outside, the love he'd felt a sham. "You used me. You never had any intention of breaking up with Rocco. Only I guess the joke is on you now that he found out we fucked. Let me guess, he dumped your ass."

"Hardly. That was my freebie."

"Your what?"

"We both had one. A last hurrah before the wedding."

"If you both agreed to cheat, why did he kick the shit out of me?" And why couldn't he go back to sleep? Because this shit was making him hurt even worse.

"What can I say? He's a jealous man. I had to reassure him he was the better lover."

Well, that was a low blow. With the heat of lust extinguished, he looked at her and wanted to slap himself for being stupid. Blame the alcohol for not seeing her clearly before.

He couldn't help the bitter tone of his words. "You're mediocre yourself."

Her expression turned frosty. "You don't have to be a jerk about it."

"I'm the one lying in a hospital bed, which your fiancé put me in because you're both assholes."

"If you're going to be like that, then I'm done here." An indignant reply to her own perfidy.

How dare she act the victim in this? And how could he have been so fucking dumb?

"So long, Melinda. *Do* let the door hit you on the way out."

She wasn't the only visit he endured that day.

Rocco's father was next, a grim but usually fair man, unless it came to his son.

The moment Bruce entered the hospital room, he said, "You've placed me in a fine pickle with your actions, Asher."

It shouldn't have surprised Asher he'd be getting the blame. The unfairness made him uncharacteristically sharp. "How about we discuss how your son and his coward friends jumped me? Wasn't even close to a fair fight." Asher might be in the wrong; however, that didn't excuse Rocco's methods.

Bruce rubbed his jaw. "What the boy did wasn't right. He and I will be having a talk about how to conduct a proper challenge. But can you blame him? You screwed his fiancée."

"Only because she told me she was done with Rocco."

"Shouldn't have mattered." Bruce slashed the air. "Guy code says you don't fuck your friends' current or ex partners."

"We're not friends." Never had been.

"Doesn't matter. You belong to the same Pack. You should have walked away."

"I thought she was my true mate."

"Is that the bullshit excuse you're going to use?" Bruce barked. "You seduced her."

"No, I fucking didn't. I told her to break things

off with Rocco if she wanted to be with me. She came to me and said it was over. That she loved me. Turns out it was some kind of deal she had with Rocco. A last chance to fuck someone else before she marries your son." He wasn't about to lie to protect her.

"Doesn't fucking matter. You should have never even talked to her knowing she belonged to another man. And this isn't the first time you've been caught fucking people you shouldn't, Asher Donovan."

Bruce might have a small point there. There'd been his grade twelve math teacher. Totally mutual, and he was technically eighteen when it happened and already set to graduate. Then there was that landscaping crew he worked with that next summer. The boss and his wife were technically separated at the time.

At the same time, there was no actual law that stated a man couldn't fuck whoever he liked, whether in a relationship or not.

"Would you feel better if, from now on, I promise to only date women outside our Pack? Hell, I'll even promise to stick to humans." He'd get into less trouble that way.

"That's not enough. I can't have you around anymore. You'll have to leave."

"Hold on a fucking second, you're banishing me?" Astonishment hued his query

"You can't stay. How is Rocco supposed to hold his head high with the man who cuckolded him still around?" Bruce held out-of-fashion views when it came to relationships.

"Are you even listening to yourself? You're kicking me out because Rocco's lying fiancée wanted not just the cake but the pie, too." He stopped short of calling her a nasty name.

"My decision is final." Bruce's firm statement on it. And absolute bullshit. A clear case of a father favoring his asshole of a son. Not a surprise. Bruce might be a fair alpha when it came to everyone else, but he had a blind spot where Rocco was concerned.

Asher wanted to launch himself from the bed and show Bruce exactly what he thought of his edict. He swallowed the anger. "Where am I supposed to go?"

"That's your problem."

"What of my mom and sister?"

"They're welcome to stay."

A small consolation. "Am I at least allowed to visit?"

"Not until you've mated or married."

In other words, never.

There was no point arguing, and quite honestly,

Asher had no interest in seeing Rocco and the duplicitous Melinda, so he left. Mis mom and sister cried, but ultimately, they had no choice. He was twenty-three, a grown man who could make his own path in the world.

He wandered for a while before ending up working in Northern Alberta, which was where he ran into Amarok, another wolf and outcast, who took one look at Asher and said, "If you need a place to stay, we've got room on the ranch."

Asher found a new home. A new family. But he made a vow long before that he would never get wasted or be fooled by love again.

ONE

Y*EARS LATER*...

A mighty pounding at the door drew Asher's attention. He debated answering, given the last time a stranger came knocking, his friend, Rok—short for Amarok—got mated. What if answering the door was the equivalent of catching the bouquet?

Instead, Asher helped himself to one of Poppy's epic cupcakes. Waiting until later wasn't an option. Even blinking wasn't recommended, as Poppy's baked confectionaries had been known to disappear.

"You gonna answer that?" Lochlan groused from his spot at the table.

"Why don't you?"

"Because I don't like people."

An honest reply, and the opposite of Asher. "I

do, usually." *Bang. Bang.* "But that's some angry knocking."

"Yup."

It also tickled his curiosity. Asher moved to the hall and stared nervously at the solid wood door. Which wasn't like him.

"Open this door before I call the cops!" hollered a woman. "Meadow! You in there? I've come to rescue you."

His brows rose. Whoever it was appeared acquainted with their Alpha's new mate. Who could it be? Because Meadow didn't have a sister.

"Would you fucking answer it already?" Lochlan hollered from the kitchen.

Asher swung it open to see a tall brunette with flashing angry eyes.

"Where's Meadow?" snapped the stranger without preamble.

"Around here somewhere," was his cautious reply.

"Are you Amarok?"

"Who's asking?"

"Her best friend, Val, asshole. What have you done with her?"

Asher perused Val up and down. Her heaving bosom. Her flushed cheeks. The shaking fist.

It hit him like lightning. A tightening of his groin.

Tremor in his soul. A bolt of knowing that had his eyes widening.

Mine, oh, mine.

Uh-oh.

He now understood why Rok had slammed the door in Meadow's face the first time they met. Panic filled him. This couldn't be happening. This angry human couldn't be his mate. He was supposed to live a lonely bachelor life.

Yet there she stood, maybe five nine-ish inches of bristling woman with a slim figure, olive complexion, and a firm shove as she pushed past him to step into the house.

And what did his dumb ass do to stop her?

Nothing.

A man never laid hands on a woman. Asher didn't care if today's world demanded he treat them as he would a guy. He just couldn't. He held open doors for women. Let them in front of him in lines—which often times meant he waited twice as long. Stood until they were seated first. And always spoke respectfully—to a gal's face, at least. With the guys, he tended to be a little loose with his language.

"Meadow!" Val bellowed, entering the living room.

"She's not in the house," Asher declared, sauntering in her stormy wake. The stories he'd heard of her from Meadow hadn't mentioned her anger issues.

"Then where is she?" Val spat as she whirled.

"Probably playing with her beaver again, ma'am." He said it with a straight face.

The woman gaped at him for a minute. It wasn't the dimpled innuendo she reacted to but the last part. "I am too young to be a ma'am, asshole."

The vulgar word lifted the corner of his lip. "Well then, what should I call you? Last I heard, darling, honey, sweetheart, and babe were off the list."

"My name is Valencia Berlusconi, dickwad."

"The famous Val," he said with a nod of his head. "Meadow's mentioned you."

"Did she mention I'm a black belt? So don't you try any cult business with me, or I will drop you," she threatened.

"Cult business?'" He couldn't help an inquiring lilt.

"How else to explain why my best friend went away for a few weeks and suddenly decided she wasn't coming home because she's marrying some backwoods mountain man."

"Not hard to explain. She fell in love."

Val snorted. "It's lust, not love, which is why I'm here."

"Oh, it's love all right." It might seem too fast and impossible to a human, and yet to the Were, of which Amarok and Asher belonged? They could love many in their lifetime, but there was only ever one true mate, and once they met, they couldn't bear to be apart.

Please let me be wrong about her. Valencia didn't seem the type to let a man enjoy alone-time with his game system, a headset, a case of beer, and pretzels.

Valencia's lip curled. "Love. Ha!"

"I agree. Alas, they're of a different opinion."

"I'll fix that," she threatened.

"Planning to crash the wedding?" he asked.

"More like stop it before it happens." The whirl-wind went from the living room to the dining room, where she briefly halted at the sight of the massive table and the benches on either side. "Just how many people live in your commune?"

"Thirteen now that Meadow's here. Soon to be fourteen once Astra pops out her baby."

"Whose baby is it?" she asked rather accusingly.

"Bellamy's—her husband—so you can get your panties out of their knot, princess."

"Who says I wear panties?"

"Look at us with something in common," he replied.

She glanced at him, then lower. He reacted

because, hello, he was a fucking man. It helped she was hot, quite possibly his mate, and he was having more fun than expected. But at the same time, he remembered the last time he'd fallen quick and hard for a woman. It cost him his home and his family. He'd not seen the first since he'd left. As for the latter, talking over the phone and messaging just weren't the same as being able to see his mom and sister in person.

Val's lips curved in a wicked smile of warning before she said, "I hope you get it caught in your zipper."

He winced. "That's just plain cruel, princess."

"Wash out your ears, dumbass. My name is Valencia," was her retort as she entered the kitchen, empty of Lochlan and the cupcakes. Bastard!

Rather than flee, Asher followed. "Valencia. Sounds Italian."

"Very. And before you ask, no, my family doesn't belong to the mob. But"—she turned a wicked smile on him—"I do have connections, so don't piss me off."

"Wait, this isn't pissed off?" he asked, genuinely curious given her rampage thus far.

Her smile was much too sweet as she said, "This is me showing loving concern for my friend."

"A friend who's down by the dam. I can show you the way if you'd like."

"How far is it? I'm not really dressed to go traipsing in the dirt." She glanced down at her trendy short boots with their two-inch heels, which led to him giving her long, lean legs in slim-fitting jeans a glance. The blouse, a crisp white linen, was tucked into her pants, and over it, she wore a Sherpa-lined vest. Very attractive and utterly impractical.

And possibly pantyless, which he found interesting given he could see the outline of a bra. Who wore a confining bra but no undies?

"Stop staring," she demanded, stomping past him to return to the front porch.

Hard to deny given he'd done nothing but look at her since she arrived. He should escape now while he could.

He joined her outside.

Valencia stood with her hands on her hips and glared at the forest. If she could have, he'd bet she'd have mown it down for a clearer view.

"Relax, princess. Meadow should be back soon. Can I offer you a beverage?" he asked.

"As if I'm that dumb. Is that how you conned her? Did your friend drug her into thinking she was in love?"

He leaned against the wall of the house, arms crossed, to drawl, "Why are you convinced they're not in love? I know you've spoken with her."

"Because Meadow might be naïve, but she isn't rash. This is the woman who spent a year price shopping her car before buying it."

Since Asher couldn't exactly tell this human about the mating bond, he had to rely on something she might believe. "It was love at first sight."

She let out a snort. "Again, I'm not dumb. I am well aware this Amarok scam artist hated her the first time they met. I heard all about it."

"You know what they say about love and hate."

"Don't give me that line of crap."

"Fine, then it's fate."

"Like fuck it is."

He arched a brow. "You don't believe in fated mates?"

"No," she huffed.

Funny, he would have sworn she was lying.

TWO

VALENCIA FLAT-OUT LIED TO THE HANDSOME man talking to her about love.

Why lie to a stranger? Because, for one, he'd discomfited her from the moment he opened the door, a blond Adonis with an easy smile and teasing nature who didn't cower before her accusations. Instant attraction had her disliking him on sight.

Val knew better than to fall for a pretty face or flirting words. She'd made that mistake in college. Fallen for the bullshit and thought herself in love.

Wrong. Gerry took not only her savings jar, her stash of junk food, and her car but also her last ounce of trust in men.

Lust wasn't love, and lust had an expiry date, which was why she'd come rushing when Meadow told her she was getting hitched to a stranger. A man

Meadow barely knew and planned to wed within a month of meeting.

Val had fully expected Meadow's parents to agree with her that their daughter was rushing into things, but Mr. and Mrs. Fields—unrelated to the cookies—were delighted their daughter had found someone, especially given they worried about her being alone since they'd moved closer to the coast. It was up to Val to ensure her best friend since kindergarten wasn't making a mistake, and now it seemed Val would have to watch herself to ensure she didn't fall into the same trap.

"What's your name?" she asked the blond hottie, hoping for something she could dislike.

"Asher Donovan, at your service." He tipped an imaginary hat. He'd look epic in a wide-brimmed Stetson. It would match the plaid shirt stretched over broad shoulders and low, hip-hugging jeans.

"You work and live here?"

"Yup." He pointed to a small building with white vinyl siding, a door, and a single large window. "That's my place."

"It's a shed."

His lips quirked. "A little more elaborate than that. Fully insulated with a wood stove, a bathroom, and a giant bed."

He would have to mention that. "I guess it's

perfect for a man-child who had to leave his mother's basement but couldn't find a real place to live."

Another person might have been offended. He laughed and then fired right back. "Let me guess, you've got a fancy condo with sleek modern lines, a gourmet kitchen, and a walk-in closet for all your shoes."

Her turn to smirk. "Try renovated Victorian with wood trim in every room and a farmhouse-style kitchen."

"Ah, you're that kind of princess."

"What's that supposed to mean?"

Rather than reply, he pointed. "They're almost here."

A glance at the woods showed Meadow finally returning. At least it looked like Meadow. Val blinked, yet her friend remained positively glowing from her sparkling eyes to her wide smile directed at the man by her side holding her hand. A handsome guy, bigger and more masculine than Meadow usually dated. More Val's style. She could see the appeal.

When Amarok's gaze met hers, she stiffened. Because, while he might have had a soft expression for Meadow, it was stone cold for Val.

She could almost see the warning in his gaze.

Don't take my Meadow away. He made it clear he didn't like Val being here.

Meadow, however, was ecstatic. "Val! Oh my god. What are you doing here?" The squeal emerged as Meadow raced for a hug.

Val met her halfway and hugged her best friend fiercely. Despite having an extensive family, Val liked very few people in the world. Loved even fewer.

"I can't believe you drove out here," Meadow babbled.

"What else did you expect when you announced you were getting married in two weeks?" Two weeks. This Amarok was really racing to tie the knot. Why? On paper he seemed well off, especially in comparison to Meadow. So why the rush?

"I know it's crazy, but once you meet Rok, you'll understand. He's my perfect mate." Meadow beamed in his direction as he neared enough to give Val a friendly nod at odds with his initial glare.

"You must be Valencia. I've heard a lot about you. Amarok Fleetfoot." He held out his hand.

Val tested the firmness of his grasp. "Call me Val. After all, you're marrying my best friend, which means we'll be spending lots of time together."

"How long can you stay?" Meadow asked, hands clasped, bouncing on the balls of her feet.

"I took the next two weeks off so I could be here for you."

It was Asher who drawled, "Now, now, princess. Don't be shy. Tell her the real reason you're here. That you think we're some kind of hippie commune who've drugged Meadow into wanting to marry Rok's grumpy ass. As if there's a drug strong enough to do that." Asher glanced at Val and shrugged. "To be honest, none of us get the attraction either."

"Asher! You're such a brat." Meadow giggled and then smiled up at Amarok. "He's perfect."

"Gag." Val and Asher both said it at the same time before looking at each other. A reluctant smile teased her lips.

"I agree. Doe might need glasses," Rok declared, but he said it with a softness that belied his appearance.

"So, now that I'm here, why don't you show me what you've got planned so far?" Val asked, wanting to separate her best friend from Rok at least long enough to see if she really was drug free. She'd never seen Meadow this happy.

"Ooh, yes, I could use your input. Nova, Poppy, and Astra have been helping me out, but they never saw my binder."

Ah yes, their wedding binder, with clippings of dresses and hairstyles. From a young age, they'd planned their perfect day. Meadow burned hers with Val in solidarity the day Val gave up on love. "Did you tell them about the dog tuxedos we'd planned?"

"The what?" Asher coughed.

Meadow laughed. "At the time, I was obsessed with Bichons, and I'd seen one dressed up for a wedding, bow tie and all."

Rok's face got the oddest expression. "I need to go check on the alpacas."

To which Asher laughed. "Can you imagine having them at the ceremony wearing ties?"

"Don't they spit?" Valencia frowned.

"Not alpacas," growled Rok as he stalked off. "Asher! Come."

"Woof." The blond hottie winked at her before trotting to join his friend, leaving Valencia alone with Meadow.

"Have you met anyone, yet?" Meadow asked, leading the way inside.

Val shook her head as she followed. "Just the pretty boy."

Meadow glanced over her shoulder with a frown. "You think he's attractive?"

"Duh. Have you seen him?"

"He's cute, I guess. I never really noticed because of Rok, who is just mmm..." Meadow hummed, and Val's brows lifted.

"You really like him, don't you?"

"It's more than that, Val. Like I told you on the phone, finding him filled a missing part of me that I didn't know I needed."

"Which is cool, but I will admit I'm kind of worried at how fast you're moving on it. I mean, marriage? Why not date for a while?"

"I know it seems crazy"—Meadow turned and clasped her hands—"but I swear, I know what I am doing. This is what I want."

Val couldn't destroy that shining expression, so she nodded. "Okay. But be aware that if he does a thing to hurt a single hair on your head, I will cement his feet and drop him in a lake."

At that, Meadow laughed. "You're so dramatic."

More like entirely serious. Hurt the best friend that was like a sister and Val would do time to get revenge.

THREE

Asher stood outside with Rok as the women went inside.

"Have you warned everyone we've got a human on the premises?" Rok asked softly.

"She barely arrived. But guess I should 'cause it doesn't sound as if she's leaving until after the wedding."

"Meadow warned me her friend might come earlier."

"Val doesn't seem too happy her BFF is getting hitched," Asher noted.

At that, Rok shrugged. "Can't say as I blame her. From the outside, it does look like we're jumping into things."

"True. It's not as if we can explain the mating bond." That sense of meeting the right person and knowing they were your future.

Like the woman inside.

Maybe Asher was mistaken about Val. Still, he asked, "When did you know for sure Meadow was your mate?"

"Always did. Problem was my stubbornness in accepting it."

"Weren't you worried she wouldn't? The feeling isn't the same for humans."

"No, but at the same time, there is something there. Call it an awareness or a level of connection. It has her in tune with me enough that she knows when to come outside to greet me after I've done a day's work." Rok glanced at him. "Why the questions?"

"Nothing. Just curious." He should have known better than to hide anything from his Alpha.

"What happened? Did you meet someone?"

"Just our new guest."

He said nothing more, and neither did Rok for a second before he chuckled. "You poor bastard."

"What's that supposed to mean?"

"Just that it's kind of funny that you're Mr. I'm Not Settling Down With Anyone, and yet you're fated to be with one that will keep you on your toes."

"Hasn't happened yet."

"It will." Rok's firm assurance.

"Don't be so sure. I don't get the impression she

likes me. Or you. Or nature for that matter." Although her large SUV was built for the outdoors, even as it was brand new and, he'd bet, loaded with features inside.

"Wanna hear something even funnier? Doe says Val hates dogs. With a passion. Claims they're smelly, gross beasts."

Asher stared at him. Then the house. Shook his head. "Of course, she does. Which means whatever I'm feeling is probably not the mating instinct."

"Are you itching to know what she's doing inside?"

"No." Lie.

"Did you want to kiss her the moment you saw her?"

"I've wanted to and have kissed many a woman I've met and found attractive."

"But none ever had you asking me about the mating bond. You can fight it, Ash, but in the end, you just won't be able to help yourself."

"I'm too young for a ball and chain," he moaned.

"You're over thirty."

"Exactly. Look at Lochlan. Forty and still single."

"Lochlan's a miserable bastard. Is that what you want?"

"If I have to be mated, why can't it be with someone happy and sweet like Meadow?"

"Because you'd be bored in a second."

"You're not bored."

"That's because I'm the kind of guy who doesn't mind snuggling and watching a movie."

"I like movies," Asher protested.

"When was the last time you managed to sit through an entire one?"

"Last Saturday."

"You slept during more than half."

"Still counts."

"You're an idiot. Keep arguing. I'm going to laugh when you fall."

"Not funny. I thought I was your right hand." He'd been given the title of Pack Beta. Darian was the other Beta and Rok's left hand. At the time Asher had been dumbstruck. The honor of it actually left him without anything smartass to reply.

"You are my right hand but also my friend. And as your friend I'm going to say, suckah!" Rok slapped him hard on the back and strode into the house still chuckling while Asher glared.

Not for long. Maybe Rok was wrong. Could be Asher was mistaken.

But just in case they weren't, he went for a run in the woods to clear his mind, only to find himself presented with a different problem.

A man dropped from a tree branch overhead. He

was dressed all in black, his hair a bright red, his features sharp. He smelled of nothing, as if he wore a non-scent. Worrisome, but given the man didn't attack, Asher opted for casual. "Hey, dude. You lost?"

"Asher Donovan. Former member of the Festivus Pack based out of Edmonton."

"Who are you?"

That arched a dark brow. "I see Mr. Fleetfoot managed to keep his mouth shut. I'm Kit."

"Kit who?"

"Just Kit. Epsilon for the Lykosium."

"Don't you mean spy?" The Lykosium were the secretive group who kept the Packs in line and ensured their laws were upheld.

"How about not a person you should be messing with." Flatly spoken.

"Why are you here? What do you want?"

"What can you tell me of the Festivus Pack?"

"Not much seeing as how I don't belong to it and haven't for a long time." He planned to keep it that way.

"Why did you leave?"

"Why does the Lykosium want to know? It's been like ten years."

"Answer the question."

"I left because I had an affair with the future

daughter-in-law of the Alpha." No point in being polite about it.

"You speak of Rocco Durante, son of Bruce Durante?"

"Yeah."

"Hospital records show you were admitted for a severe beating about ten years ago."

"The streets can be rough late at night."

The line of questioning abruptly pivoted. "Are you aware of Rocco or his father indulging in criminal activity?"

"No."

"Are you sure?"

"What is this about? Why come see me? Why not talk to someone in the Pack?"

"Because we are unsure who to trust."

The blunt truth stunned Asher for a second. "You're telling me this because..."

"Because the Lykosium have tasked me with finding out if there is anything untoward currently happening within the Festivus Pack."

"Still don't see how I'm supposed to help you."

"By returning for a visit and seeing what you can uncover."

His laughter barked. "You chose the wrong guy. I'm not welcome."

"Your family is still with that Pack. It gives you reason."

"Not without a wife, I can't. Condition of my return. Without one, Bruce would be within his right to have me severely punished."

"Pity." Kit looked put out. "I guess I'll have to tap someone else. Maybe one of the women." Kit's expression turned sly. "You have a sister, don't you?"

Asher's blood ran cold. "Leave her out of this. She just had a baby." Literally a few days ago. She'd video called him, arms cradling his new niece, Bella. Asher had the biggest stuffed wolf he could find delivered to Winnie's house.

"I don't have many options, Mr. Donovan. But I'm a nice guy. I'll give you a day or two to think about it."

"Or what?"

The enigmatic smile didn't help one bit. "Guess you'll soon find out. Oh, and don't tell anyone about my visit."

A noise from behind had him whirling to glance only for a second. By the time he turned back, the strange man had disappeared, but his threat lingered. As if Asher didn't have enough to think about.

This Kit fellow had to be insane, asking him for help. At the same time just how bad were things with his old pack that he'd even been approached?

More importantly, were his mother and sister in danger?

Asher ran hard back to the ranch, working up a good sweat. A shower freshened him, and then he dressed for dinner with the Pack—and Val. A woman he'd managed to forget since his meeting with Kit.

A woman who invaded all his senses the moment he walked into the main house and smelled her. It made his step quicken, his pulse race.

But was she happy to see him?

Without even turning around, she muttered, "Great. You're back."

FOUR

Val spent the afternoon alternating between helping Meadow with her wedding plans and spying for Asher's return. Why she watched for him she couldn't have said.

She barely paid any mind to Rok when he entered the house. Met the rest of the commune's residents throughout the afternoon. She finally put faces to the names Meadow had bombarded her with.

Nova, with her piercing and short hair, eyed Val over and said, "Straight?"

"Yes," Val's replied.

Nova said with clear regret, "What a shame."

Being a smartass, Val couldn't help but say, "If I weren't, you'd be my type."

Nova laughed, and that was that.

She met Poppy, who was a bit shyer than Nova and the person in charge of all the cooking, which she handled impressively and deliciously.

"This hot cocoa is orgasm in a cup," Val declared after one satisfying gulp.

Poppy blushed, but the very pregnant Astra seated beside her agreed. "If you think that's good, wait until you have her sugar pie."

"I'm making tartlet versions for the wedding reception," Poppy stated.

"Along with her tourtière. It is the most delicious thing I've ever had." Meadow enthused over the menu they'd planned. Although Val had to wonder at the choice of a meat pie for the main dish. It better be the fancy kind with real chunks of meat and potato and not the one with plain ol' ground beef.

Val met the grumpy Lochlan, who managed a grunt before practically running off.

Hammer, who appeared as blunt as his name.

Reece and Gary were a sweet couple, as were Astra and Bellamy.

Not the commune Val expected. While Val hated to admit it, thus far, she didn't hate anyone she'd met. But she was reserving judgment on Rok, the man who treated her best friend as if she were the most precious thing in the world.

The guy was stealing Val's BFF. It would be hard

to do dinner and a movie if Meadow lived in the boonies.

Dinnertime saw all of them gathered at the massive table with Asher down from Val, not that it stopped her from being aware of his presence. Every time he laughed, she shivered. The timbre of his voice tingled.

She did her best to keep busy conversing with others but couldn't help but sneak peeks at him. Each time, she got caught, as if he watched her, too.

After dinner, most everyone drifted off to their rooms or to check on animals. Astra, Bellamy, and Nova extended an invite to watch a movie. Meadow and Rok had a planned video call with her parents, leaving Val with a choice of being third wheel in that conversation or entertaining herself.

"I'm going for a walk," she declared.

"I'll go with you," Asher offer. "I'll protect you from the wild animals."

"I'll be fine. Meadow loaned me her safety bell." She rang it, and Asher gaped. Val held in her snicker of amusement.

"Uh, hate to break it to you, princess, but that won't stop a wolf."

She reached into her purse and pulled out a small pistol. "This will."

The expression on his face?

Admiration. "Well damn. Nice to see you're not just all good looks, princess."

"That's all you gotta say?" she asked as she tucked it into her waistband.

"Well, I could be a jerk and say the only gun you should play with is the one in my pants. But you obviously like something with a smaller grip." He winked as he held open the outside door for her.

Point for the mountain hick. He'd managed to get one up on her. Now she'd have to get him back.

She stepped outside and shivered in her vest. The temperature had dropped quite a bit since the afternoon. "How is it so freaking cold already?"

"Fall up north is different than the city. You're going to need something warmer," he declared and went inside, only to return with a plaid jacket similar to his own.

She wrinkled her nose. "I don't think so."

"Suit yourself." He draped it on the railing and headed down the steps.

Already regretting her decision to go for a walk, Val followed. She wasn't about to admit she'd changed her mind. Especially since he thought he held the upper hand.

Hitting the dirt path into the woods, she realized quickly her heeled boots weren't built for this terrain. Chin high, she silently kept pace beside him.

For about thirty seconds. "Is it me or does Amarok collect strays?"

"Cats are good for keeping the vermin population in check."

"Ha. Ha. Funny guy. You know I meant people. You're a mishmash of folks from all over."

"Yep."

"How did you all end up here?" Because this ranch was literally at the end of some hard-to-find road.

"Luck. For me, right place, right time. I met Rok when I was out of work. He happened to need an extra set of hands."

"And you like it out here?" She hugged her body, doing her best to cut the chilly evening air, wishing she'd taken the coat.

"Love it. It's peaceful and beautiful." He tilted his head back, and she followed suit to see a sky full of stars.

"Pretty, but not sure living in the boonies for quiet is worth the drive to shop."

He chuckled. "It is a bit of a trek."

"Bit? It's an hour just to that tiny town."

"You're a city girl?"

"More like suburbia because I like some space between houses."

"What do you do for work?"

"Office manager."

"Must be for a nice company given your wheels."

"I got a good deal. I've got an uncle who sells cars. What do you drive?"

"Depends on the weather. Motorbike when it's nice. I borrow Big Betty when it's not."

Her lip lifted. "That must be the gas guzzler Meadow mentioned."

"She's trying to talk Rok into swapping Big Betty for a hybrid."

Val snorted. "She tried that shit with me, too."

"You didn't cave, obviously, but Rok just might. He's head over heels for her."

It couldn't have been more obvious at dinner. "Yeah, I noticed."

"You don't approve, though."

She whirled to face him. "Meadow is my best friend, which means I'll support whatever she wants, but I'll be damned if I don't make sure he's good enough for her."

"Fair enough. What about you?"

"What about me?"

"Single? Married?" he asked in rapid fire.

"Not looking."

"Me either." That caused a stretch of silence before he said, "I hear you hate dogs."

"Damned straight I do. Smelly things. One of

them bit me as a kid. I still have the scar on my calf."
She scowled.

"That blows, but you do know most of them are pretty decent?"

"I know and don't care. I will never own a dog. Although I don't mind cats."

"Snooty fuckers if you ask me."

"I wasn't asking."

He chuckled. "You're very forthright."

"If you mean I don't take any bullshit, then you would be correct. Honesty is the best policy in all things."

"Well, in that case then, I should mention that, from the moment I've met you, I've wanted to kiss you senseless."

FIVE

He froze, waiting for Val's reply while inwardly berating himself.

Why had he said it?

Hell, why had he joined her on this walk?

He knew why. It was all he could do to keep away from her at dinner. Now they were alone, and the more time he spent time with her, the harder it was to concentrate on anything other than her.

Mine.

Fuck.

Mine.

Double fuck.

While it was dark outside, he could still see her face, the pensive look that crossed it then the sultrier softening.

"What's stopping you from kissing me?" she asked.

"Fear of being slapped." He stuck to a partial truth. What if a single kiss led to more?

"Actually, I'm more partial to kneeing the groin. It hurts more."

His balls tightened in fear, but that didn't stop him from stepping closer. "Are you going to try and maim me if I kiss you?" A kiss would tell him for sure if she was his mate. Perhaps he'd just been without a companion for too long. He certainly couldn't blame booze for the tingling within. He'd been sober since his days with Melinda.

"The maiming depends on if you're a good kisser or not."

"Well, shit. Way to give me performance anxiety," he teased.

"Do I make you nervous?" She arched a brow.

He couldn't help a lopsided grin. "Fuck yeah, you do. I mean we'll remember this first kiss for the rest of our lives."

Laughter burst free, loud and boisterous. "As if you and I will end up together."

"Why is that so funny?" For once he spoke quite seriously.

"One"—she held up a finger—"I am not interested in settling down. Two, if I were to settle down, it would be with a guy who holds a nine-to-five job in the city. Because three, this girl isn't living in the boonies."

"You say that, and yet you've not even given it a chance."

"Don't have to because I am not a girl in tune with nature."

With every word she displayed how wrong she was for Asher.

With every word his desire for her only grew.

"Maybe you could be with the right guy."

Her nose wrinkled. "Why should I change? I'm happy where I am."

"Even if Meadow is staying here?"

"There's always video chat, and while the drive is a bit long, it's doable. Although I might look into renting a helicopter to shorten the trip. I have an aunt who runs a fleet."

"What if you fell in love with a backwoods hick?" he asked, stepping closer.

Val didn't need to tilt her head to meet his gaze. "That won't happen."

"Are you sure? Because once I kiss you, there's no going back," he warned. This kiss might be the start of the end for both of them. While it would take sex to make a true claiming, the touch of their lips would be that match that ignited everything.

Again, her laughter filled the air. "Does that line really work with the girls?" Even as she mocked, she grabbed Asher and whispered against his mouth, "Let's see if you're as good as you think you are."

Their lips met, a firm press that jolted. His breath caught, and so did hers. They kissed, a passionate meld of breath and lips, heat and desire.

Their hands clutched and roamed as they embraced. Exploring. Learning. Teasing. It might have gone further if an owl hadn't hooted.

"*Who.*"

She froze and pushed away from him, eyes wide. "Who was that?"

"An owl. We're alone." Out of sight of anyone who might have seen him engaging in madness. Wait, *were* they alone? He remembered the man he'd met that day. The Lykosium spy. Did he hide in the shadows, watching?"

"It's cold out here. And dark." She whirled and began stomping in those heels—that would look great around his neck—back to the house.

He quickly caught up just in time to rescue her when her ankle twisted and she almost spilled to the ground. "Gotcha." He swept her into his arms. She fit as if she belonged, although her scowl said otherwise.

"Someone should do something about the ruts on this path," she grumbled.

"Or you could wear something a little more appropriate for the conditions."

Her lips pressed into a line. "Is this your hillbilly cult hint I should be barefoot and pregnant?"

He gaped, mostly because the thought never occurred to him, but now that she'd mentioned it, he was reminded that mated usually meant pups. But she hated dogs. Plus, he wasn't dad material. It would cut into his gaming time, of which he had precious little already given his duties on the farm. Seven days a week pretty much, at varying hours of the day.

"Speechless because I'm right?" she taunted.

"More like shocked you'd think I'd want to be around a squalling baby. I am not into kids." He said it, believed it, but had to wonder if his decision was more about not meeting the right woman to bear them.

"I'm not the mommy type either. Nor do I want a husband who thinks he can tell me what to do."

"Marriage is overrated." On that they agreed.

Was he wrong about Val being his mate? The more they spoke, the less likely it seemed they belonged together.

They exited the woods, and Val wiggled. "Put me down. I can walk."

Asher set her on her feet.

Val flung back her hair. "Thanks for the help. I guess I should go find out where my room is."

Ah yes, the other reason he'd joined her on the walk. Rok had cornered him before dinner to ask a favor.

"Speaking of room... The house is kind of full up unless you want to sleep in a crib. Rok's talking about adding on another wing and maybe a larger cottage or two. But that takes time."

Val froze and glanced at him over her shoulder, her face illuminated by the porch light. "Let me guess. I'm getting a lumpy couch."

"Actually, princess, given the length of your stay, you get to stay at Maison Asher."

"Your shed?"

"Cabin is the proper term. The trendy call it a tiny home."

"Tiny." Her nose wrinkled.

"It's that or the couch. Take your pick, princess."

"It better have clean sheets."

"And a pea under the mattress to test your royal status," he mocked.

She arched a brow. "See that it also has fresh towels." Then, with a haughty toss of her head, she clomped into the house, leaving him with an urge to chase after her.

Nope.

Not happening.

Nor would he be trying to cajole his way into bed with her.

But he might need someone to chain him to a tree to make sure he didn't break his own vow.

SIX

VAL GLANCED FOR A MIRROR TO CHECK ON THE
state of her lips. No lipstick to worry about but that
had been a fierce embrace in the woods. The kind
that left a mouth rosy and swollen.

How had that happened?

She'd meant to give Asher a quick kiss and then
brush him off. Imagined a hick like him would be bad
at it and her libido would finally calm down.

Instead, she'd almost clawed off his clothes for
outdoors sex, which she'd never done and never
would do. She preferred a bed. If it hadn't been for
that fierce-sounding bird, she would have possibly
eschewed that preference.

It astonished that she'd pushed Asher away and
he didn't force the issue. Didn't his blood rage with

heat? When he'd told her she was staying at his place, she'd almost asked if he came with it.

It would be bad to sleep with him. She'd just arrived. She couldn't afford to screw him too early, because then she'd have to deal with him until the wedding was done. Two weeks playing nice with one guy? Barely doable. How then was she supposed to resist his allure?

She ignored the blare of the television and headed for the kitchen. Poppy was seated at the counter with a laptop open.

"Studying?" Val asked, noticing the college logo at the top.

"Yeah." Poppy closed the lid. "I know I'm a little old for it."

"You're younger than me." The girl was mid-twenties according to Meadow.

"Always wanted to go to college, but...life got in the way."

"What are you studying?" Val headed for the fridge, hoping for wine. She'd had the thick-set fellow with a blunt name—Chisel or Hammer or something—bring in the case she'd brought from the city. As if she'd go two days, let alone two weeks, without a nice red.

The bottle in the fridge remained corked,

presenting the dilemma of how to open it. "Please tell me there is a bottle opener."

Poppy rescued her. "Second drawer by the stove."

"Glasses?" Valencia asked as she turned with the implement and bottle.

"By the sink. But none for me."

"Aren't you of age?"

"Yes, my disinterest is because wine is gross."

Pop. Valencia uncorked the bottle before setting it down to get glasses. "That's because you didn't have the right wine. This particular vintage is a special blend created by my Aunt Maria." She returned with two glasses and poured a few ounces in each.

Val swirled it and sniffed. "This is a real wine."

Despite her dubious expression, Poppy lifted her glass and imitated.

"To my best friend getting married." She held out her glass, and Poppy clinked.

Val knew what to expect taste-wise but enjoyed watching the surprise on Poppy's face.

"That's nice. I have no urge to spit it out."

That brought laughter. "Good wine should caress your mouth like a lover."

That caused the girl to blush bright. "I wouldn't know."

A virgin surrounded by handsome men? Given the girl also flinched and stared about abruptly at times as if afraid of being caught, Val surmised trauma. It peeved her. Who would hurt this sweet thing?

"It's time you found out then." Val poured a few more ounces in each glass.

Nova and Meadow eventually joined them, along with Astra, who drank water. A few hours and several emptied bottles later, some tipsy women went to find their beds. Darian took charge of his sister. Nova could still walk straight and wink at Val. Rok carried Meadow. While Astra took the leftover popcorn to bed.

As for Val? Her guide popped up out of nowhere to say, "Follow me, my tipsy princess."

"Fuck you. Not drunk," she slurred.

She made it to the front door, where she eyed her heeled boots sitting on the mat. Those would not be fun to walk in. She held out her arms. "Carry me."

"Handing out edicts now?" Asher asked even as he swept her into his strong grip. He didn't strain at all as he transported her from the house and down the steps.

"If you're going to call me princess, then I will act like one."

"So long as you don't scream, 'Off with his head.'"

She giggled. "It's too pretty to cut." She slapped a hand over her drunken mouth.

His chest rumbled when he chuckled. "You're fairly cute yourself."

"Ha," she snorted. "We both know I am gorgeous."

"And conceited," he added. "But to be fair, I am too."

"We're both too pretty." She sighed.

"Such a hardship," he agreed.

He stopped and fiddled with the door before bringing her into his man shed. Which, to be fair, appeared more like a bachelor apartment. A cute one. It had a potbellied stove against a wall and a massive bed across from it, covered in the thickest duvet she'd ever seen, a very chic red plaid. It went well with the wood accents inside. Although the curtained off area for his potty? That was of some concern.

Could it handle a puking woman at three in the morning?

He set her gently on the bed, the cover tugged back before he nestled her. They smelled like the kind of sheets dried outside. She'd know since they used to hang theirs as much as possible to save money.

"Mmm." She buried her face in the pillow.

"You might want to strip?" he suggested.

"Undress me," she demanded as she rolled to her back and flung out her arms.

"Nope. I know better than to obey a drunk woman."

"Not drunk."

"Oh yes you are, which means you could beg me and I will still walk away."

"I could make you stay." She grabbed at her blouse and yanked. Buttons popped, as did his eyes.

He retreated. "Good night, princess."

She might have called him back, but she passed out.

SEVEN

Forget walking, Asher ran away. Val proved to be a temptation that stretched his control. But he would never take advantage of a woman under any kind of influence.

He bolted to the house and had the shittiest night's sleep on the couch until, at three a.m., he poured himself into the hammock outside. The big blanket he'd dragged along kept him snug until that early-rising fucker, Bellamy, walked by and sent the hammock rocking.

Asher hit the porch with a thud. "I hate you." A lie. These people were family. Brothers. Sisters. Which meant they constantly bugged each other.

He'd get Bellamy later. This was probably retaliation for the empty popcorn tub he'd hidden in Bellamy's closet. Everyone knew the very pregnant

Astra liked her popped kernels best the day after. But Asher was hungry, so he ate it and then laid the blame elsewhere.

Bellamy could handle it. Astra was, after all, his wife. Asher, though, didn't want to make Astra mad. What if she went into labor? Or told him he couldn't be called uncle?

Given Asher wouldn't be going back to sleep, he stood and stretched, keeping a sly eye on his cabin. Val had not yet come out.

Lochlan emerged from his cabin and strode across the yard.

Asher skipped down the steps to meet him. "Mind if I borrow your shower?"

"Because yours is..."

"Being used by our guest."

Lochlan grunted. "Bring your own towel and soap."

Asher brought his own clothes, too, after digging them out of the clean pile in the laundry room. Showered and dressed, he felt almost ready to face the world. He'd conquer it after breakfast. He strode into the ranch house and headed for the kitchen. Entered it and saw the most perfect ass in the air. His hand lifted to smack it.

Val eyed him between her legs. "Don't even think of it, cowboy."

"You can't stop me from thinking it."

"Slap it and die," she warned, grabbing the scrunchie she'd dropped.

"Slap mine and I will have what the French call the le *petit mort*."

Val whipped upward, her hair a curtain that flew and settled around her, giving her a tumbled-out-of-bed look. She grabbed her loose hair and with a quick twist of her scrunchie had it pulled back from her face.

"How did you sleep?" he asked.

"Passably."

"Were you lonely?" He couldn't help but tease.

"I have a cure for loneliness. It's called my hand." She winked.

He couldn't help but shift in her direction. "I could do better."

"Spoken with such confidence. Are you really that sure? Most men think they know what makes a woman feel good. But guess what? I often have to finish myself."

"Because you weren't with the right man."

"Are you saying you are?"

"I guarantee pleasure."

She stood on tiptoe, so her next words brushed his mouth. "I'm good for the day."

He groaned. "Killing me here, princess."

"Don't die until I'm gone. I'm not in the mood to dispose of another body." Her parting shot as she left him for the dining room.

He gaped. Another body? Could she get any sexier?

He gravitated toward her, entering the dining room almost on her heels. They had it to themselves.

Poppy had laid out a buffet: pancakes, sausages, bacon, scrambled eggs, and fruit, along with coffee and juice.

"Hash browns. Hot damn, my favorite." Val took two, along with some fruit and bacon.

She sat on the bench, and he took the spot across from her. Given she appeared determined to ignore him, he made it impossible.

"How was your night?" he asked.

"Excellent. Your bed is very comfy. Although you will have to change the sheets when I leave. Things might have gotten a little wet." A purred reply that had him hardening.

Hopefully she didn't guess his sudden urge to sniff them like a perv. Fuck. What was wrong with him? He needed to get himself under control.

"Speaking of wet, did you enjoy the detachable showerhead? It has multiple settings."

Her turn to have her mouth round before she

caught herself. "I'll be sure to let you know once I try."

He might just die. He ate for a minute, concentrating on the crunch and flavor of his food.

Nova arrived in the meantime, along with Hammer. The general conversation allowed him to hide behind the occasional dig at Hammer.

Meadow's flush-cheeked arrival and Rok's pleased one meant a bit more chaos. Soon as Asher could, he escaped, using the pretext of running into town to grab supplies. Not exactly untrue, it just wasn't quite urgent. He took his sweet time, doing a bit of shopping. Having lunch. He even stopped by the post office and grabbed the mail while he was there. On the way back was when he ran into trouble.

He'd borrowed Rok's Big Betty, who coughed, spewed some smoke, and died about twenty kilometers from home. Fuck. He'd have to walk because, with a human on premises, no going four-legged.

Unless he could score a ride. His phone didn't cooperate. The signal out here, even with satellite, could be tricky. He got out of his truck and stood on the hood, holding his phone up, hoping the text he sent to Rok was received.

Ping.

He brought his phone back down and grunted at

the delivered notification and the thumbs-up reply. Rok would send someone to get him.

He parked his ass on the hood, legs dangling, to wait. He could have groaned when he saw who they sent.

"You?"

Val arched a brow as she hopped out of the driver's seat of her SUV. "I'm sorry, would you prefer a beer-bellied redneck who wants to overcharge you for a tow?"

"How are you and your toy supposed to help?"

"For one, my Grand Cherokee has a 5.7 Hemi. It can tow over seven thousand pounds."

He whistled. "Okay, that's impressive. But why would you need that much power?"

"My boat."

He blinked. "Your boat. You mean like a kayak or something?" Wasn't that what city women liked?

"It's an eighteen-foot bowrider. Great for river boating or the lake."

"Hold on. You drive a real boat. For pleasure?"

She rolled her eyes. "Why else?"

"It just doesn't seem like you. I thought you hated the outdoors."

"I hate the boonies. Give me a luxury chalet in Banff with a hot tub and a stone fireplace and I am in heaven."

"But you don't like nature."

"Being close to it is not my thing. Looking at it? Totally different. I love a screened porch or a nice big window with a view."

"That's not how you're supposed to use the outdoors."

"Maybe you don't, but I do. Now, are you done questioning my vacation choices? Let's hook you up. And by us, I mean you. These nails don't do manual labor."

There she went back to being a princess. A sexy one that he was about to order around.

"Move your SUV so the ass end is close to the front of Betty. Did Rok at least give you the T-bar?"

"That dirty thing in the back? I made them put a tarp down first."

Asher grabbed it and hooked it to the hitch before dropping the winch that lowered the bar to hook onto the truck's front axle. Cranking a creaky handle lifted it off the ground. He placed the truck's transmission in neutral before getting into her passenger seat.

The heated padding was nice, but he found himself more distracted by having her scent surrounding him. It might be too much for him to handle. He rolled down his window.

"Hot in here," he muttered.

"Only if you're a polar bear."

He bristled. "As if I'd be something so mangy."

"Excuse me. What are you then? A prickly porcupine?"

He almost said wolf. He chose to play it safe. "You going to be okay to drive? It can be tricky with a load on the back."

"You senile? I just told you I pull a boat with my truck."

"This is not a truck."

"Semantics. And yes, I'll be fine. My grandpa had me run a tow route in the summers when I was in college." She hit the gas and got them moving.

"Do you have family members in every industry?" Because she'd mentioned more than a few already.

"Yes."

"Practical."

"Annoying. If I need something and don't deal with them, they can get so pissy. But at the same time, I'm not happy that my aunt in Toronto and my uncle in Frederickville expect me to use them but don't offer a family deal."

"Bastards."

"Right?" To his surprise, she glanced at him and asked, "You have family?"

"Everyone at the ranch."

"I meant blood family."

"Mom and a sister. But I haven't visited in a while."

"Why not?"

"Long drive."

"That's not the whole reason," she surmised.

"Because it's easier for them if I'm not around." Then realizing it sounded pathetic and whiny he added, "We text, video chat and stuff, though.

"Must be nice and quiet. I thought when my parents died I'd be done with the whole be nice and social thing. But no. My extended family are always in my face no matter how many times I yell at them to go away."

"You don't sound as if you like them."

"Most are crooks and jerks."

"Is that why you're friends with Meadow?"

Her lips quirked. "She is pretty straight and narrow when it comes to things. Someone had to keep her from getting hurt."

"Rok will do that for her. The guy loves her to pieces."

"'For now. It just seems too fast."

"Because when you meet the right person, you know." That kiss last night with Val had only made things worse for him.

"Lust is not love."

"No, it's not. But it is often an indicator. Tell me, princess, now that you've had a taste of me, do you want more?"

"I'm driving."

"Not an answer."

"Fine. I don't feel an urge. You were okay."

His ego didn't like that. "That kiss was more than okay."

"Go ahead and think that if it makes you feel better." She shrugged, acting nonchalant, and yet he heard the way her breathing quickened, sensed her heating. But most damning of all, he smelled her arousal.

"So my kiss didn't do it. What about my touch?"

"What about it?"

"Did you like it?"

Her breathe caught before she huffed. "No."

"Liar."

"What makes you think I'm lying?"

"Because I know you're wet. I know you masturbated thinking of me."

The brakes screamed and the SUV jolted as she pulled over.

Her eyes flashed. "I did not think of you."

"Hell yeah you did. Don't worry, princess, your lust for me is natural. You can't help yourself. Even better you don't have to suffer. Let me ease your desire."

Her mouth rounded. "I am not having sex with you."

"No sex needed, seeing as how I'm quite good with my fingers." Good enough she might reciprocate and they could both have their lust assuaged without doing the horizontal tango.

"Ew. That's gross. I can't believe you said that."

"Is there a nice way of saying I want to finger fuck you?" Yes, he was purposefully crude because her arousal drove him mad. Either they did something to ease the ache or she needed to push him away.

"How about you say nothing at all?"

"It was simply an offer."

"A vulgar and inappropriate one."

"You're right. It was. Would you like to slap me?" He proffered a cheek and a grin.

"You think you're so cute and smart; meanwhile you're smug and really crude. An obvious hillbilly with no manners. Do you really think you stand a chance with me?"

She hit him hard and below the belt because he did think himself cute and smart. But was he fooling himself?

He might have doubted himself more if he didn't

smell the truth. "Me think you doth protest too much, princess. Because I know you're wet."

"Am not."

"No? So you're not intrigued by me getting close to you?" He leaned in. "Sharing another kiss while my hand inches up your thigh?"

"Do you really think I'm that easy? Try it," she dared.

He accepted. "You feel nothing when I put my hand here?" He gripped her thigh before sliding his hand slightly higher.

Her breath hitched. "Nothing."

"And my kiss? You said it was horrible, right?" He breathed the words warmly on her lips.

"Maybe it was okay."

"How about we try again?" He slanted his mouth over hers and kissed her. Sucked at her lower lip as if it were candy. Played with her tongue and slid his hand to the vee of her thighs. The heat of her burned even through fabric. He pressed his palm against her as he kissed her.

Rubbing.

Pushing.

She made soft noises in his mouth, and her hips thrust against his hand. Her mini orgasm had him clenching tight. Her responsiveness was so perfect, and yet she pushed him away?

"We should get going before they send out another rescue team." She put the SUV in drive.

"I don't think we're done."

"I am." A smug reply.

His throbbing cock whined, but the male within thrust out his chest with pride.

"You going to persist in telling me that was just okay?" His voice emerged a little rough.

"Will you feel better if I upgrade your kiss to nice?"

"Nice?" It emerged harsh. Did she not feel the same boiling heat?

"Next time"—her gaze dropped—"try harder."

The teasing words left him throbbing but also strangely satisfied. Because he'd discovered one very important thing.

Val couldn't resist him.

The problem was he also had no defense against her. If they had sex, he'd be done for. A goner. Mated for life. The idea almost saw him bailing out of the SUV to run howling into the woods.

Instead, he wondered when he could kiss her again.

EIGHT

WHY CAN'T I RESIST HIM?

Val meant to be aloof with Asher, even as she felt anything but. The man made her so freaking hot, and ever since that first kiss, she'd not been able to forget.

And now? He'd made her come without taking off any of her clothes.

That wasn't supposed to happen. She wasn't supposed to be falling for him. Unlike Meadow, she knew she couldn't live here in the woods full time. Already she felt herself getting antsy. Two days down with at least twelve more to go before the wedding.

She might not make it.

"Give you a penny for your thoughts."

"Try a twenty and maybe we can start talking."

He chuckled. "You are something else, princess."

"Excuse me?"

"You misunderstand. I mean that it's a good thing. You're forthright. Bold. You don't pretend anything."

"I don't like lies."

He grimaced. "Neither do I, but some are necessary."

"What do you lie about?"

"Not my cock size because I know you're wondering."

She glanced at his lap then his face quickly. Her lip pulled at the corner. "I know exactly what to expect." Wanted it. She might have only met him the day before, but she would definitely be sleeping with Asher. Because damn... The man pushed every single one of her buttons.

But she hated that he knew it, which was why she kept playing hot and cold. She didn't want to be too easy. Let him work for it. Let him—

His hand skimmed her thigh before giving it a squeeze. "You might want to ease up before the last corner. This time of year, the geese are in the area and like to fuck around on the road."

She slowed down a little too much, wanting to draw out the sensation of him touching her. Remembering how it felt...

He leaned close as she parked in the yard to whisper, "If you need me, you just have to ask."

"What I need is to pee," she snapped, ignoring the tremble in her limbs. She practically sprinted from the truck, her current running shoes a better choice of footwear out here, if not as cute.

Inside Asher's cabin, she leaned against the door. Took a deep breath. Almost put a hand between her legs. How could she want him still?

Because that orgasm in the SUV was just an appetizer. Imagine how it would be flesh on flesh.

She quivered and ran for his bed, knowing his bathroom was too tiny to maneuver in. The pants went down. Her hand went to work. She came fast and hard thinking of him.

It didn't help. She still ached and now smelled of pussy. The removable showerhead made a fine job getting her to come again while cleaning.

She emerged smelling fresh and calm, hormones under control. Dressing casually, she headed for the ranch house, noticing the big red truck no longer hooked to her vehicle and no one in sight.

She found Nova at the kitchen counter sorting through a pile of mail while Asher nursed a mug at the table.

"You've got mail," Nova declared, frisbeeing a letter at Asher.

He snared it with an impressive dive out of his chair that had him rolling and popping up from the floor. He tore open the envelope, and his face went through a few emotions: happy, sad, then stoic resignation.

"What's wrong?" Val asked, getting close for a peek.

"Nothing," he lied, but when he would have stuffed the missive into his pocket, Val snatched it and read.

"It's an invitation to a christening. Who's Winnie? Your baby mama?" It emerged curt.

"You jealous?" Asher teased.

"No!" Val huffed, even as she battled annoyance.

"No need to worry, princess, my heart still belongs to you. The baby is my sister's."

"Congrats on being an uncle."

"Thanks."

"When do you leave to see the baby?" she asked, sliding into a seat, noticing the plate of cookies on the table. Only two were left with some crumbs.

"Probably never unless Winnie brings her to the ranch."

"Why is it up to her? You're pretty out there for a visit, especially for someone with a child," she remarked.

"I am aware; however, I'm not exactly welcome home."

"You the bad seed of the family?"

The dimple should have warned her. "According to the family gossips, a huge whore."

Her brow lifted. "True?"

"Yes. But in my defense, I wasn't the one doing most of the seducing."

She could see it. With his looks, women probably threw themselves at him. "So you have a reputation. I don't see why that's stopping you from going back. Are you afraid someone is going to call you a slut?"

"More like my concerned cousin will try to rearrange my face and break a few of my bones again. He's still ornery that I slept with the woman he took as his wife."

"You cuckolded your cousin?"

"Distant cousin, and at the time, they weren't married."

"Not cool."

"In my defense, she told me they broke up."

She bit her lower lip. "Oh. That's a shit thing for her to do." But she could understand why. Asher wasn't like other men.

"Now you see why I can't return."

"Not really. Just don't tell the cousin you're coming."

"He'd find out. And I don't know about you, but I rather like my face the way it is."

"Bruises will heal. Stop being a wuss. Let your cousin punch you a few times and problem solved." Val had a solution.

"If only it were that simple. Rocco's not the type to have a fair fight, and there's a good chance I could end up really hurt. Maybe dead."

She arched a brow. "And I thought my family was bad. Still, this is your niece and your sister we're talking about. There has to be a way for you to go see her and the baby."

"There is one, but it's ridiculous. I have to be married."

Her laughter emerged too boisterous to be contained. "You're too much a player to settle down."

"I agree. Hence my dilemma."

"You could fake it."

He snorted. "It won't work."

"Why not?"

"Because they'll expect to see my wife. Kind of hard to fabricate one."

Nova, who'd been sifting the mail this entire time, jumped in to say, "Actually, the woman's got a point. A fake wife is the perfect solution."

"Are you volunteering?" was his amused reply.

To which Valencia had to restrain an urge to interfere. Jealousy had no place here.

"As if anyone would believe I could be your bitch." Nova made a face.

"Then guess I'm kind of screwed, because I doubt Rok will let me borrow Meadow and Astra is way too pregnant."

"I could do it."

Two pairs of eyes swung Val's way.

"You?" He didn't hide the skeptical note.

"Yeah me." She scowled. "Don't look so surprised and don't think it's because I'm interested in you or anything. I just think it's pathetic you're too afraid to go see your sister and the baby. If it takes being your fake wife to do it, then so be it. It's just over in Edmonton. Which actually works because, while we're there for the christening, I'll grab a few wedding things. Might even get a bachelorette party wrangled for my BFF."

"Ooh, if you get strippers, don't forget a pretty girl for me." Nova winked.

"Strippers are outdated. We'd be hitting a casino and seeing if we can win enough to pay for her honeymoon."

"Did you say casino?" Meadow suddenly appeared. "You know I love those machines with the handles that spin the fruit thingies."

"And what the boss's future wife wants, she should get." Nova clapped her hands. "Guess Val and Asher are going on a road trip."

Hold on a second. What? Val opened her mouth to refuse. She should have never suggested anything.

Asher beat her to the punch. "I'm not going."

"Why not? You think I'm not good enough to be your wife?" Val attacked.

"What?" Meadow blinked. "Did I miss something?"

"Asher can't go home until he's hitched. Val volunteered to help him." Nova grinned wide as she said, "By the power invested in me, by some website I can't recall the name of, I now declare Asher and Val fake husband and wife."

"It won't work," Asher said.

"Do you want to see your family or not?" Val snapped.

"Yeah."

"Then stop arguing and start obeying, *husband.*" It gave Val a strange thrill to say it, and his face went through all kinds of expressions before settling on amused.

"Guess I better get used to my ball and chain ordering me around."

And with that, plans were made for them to leave the following morning. They had only a little bit of time to figure out a few things to make this work.

Given they'd need a plausible backstory, she invited him back to his own cabin after dinner. She sat cross-legged on the bed, while he got the armchair. The cabin seemed much smaller with him in it. She resisted the temptation to pluck the comforter and eyed him straight on.

"I was thinking, do we have to be married, or will a fiancée do? Because it shows intent but, if later on you say we've broken up, isn't as big of a deal."

"Are you divorcing me already?" He put a hand to his heart.

"Just trying to make it less of a lie."

"Having second thoughts? I know you're not into subterfuge."

"Never said I wasn't into pretending. I just hate being bullshitted by people I'm supposed to trust."

"Fair enough. You do realize, though, that you're asking me to lie to my mother and sister."

"You could tell them the truth. This would be just to convince your cousin or whoever else might tattle on you."

"Which means not telling my mom and sister. If we want this to look authentic, then we need to be convincing enough to fool my mother and sister into thinking we're actually a couple. I don't think you can do it."

"Me? Exactly what are you insinuating?"

"You'd have to be nice to me."

"I am nice to you," she snapped.

He arched a brow. "Do you even realize how much you bark at me?"

"Just because I'm assertive doesn't make me a bitch."

"Never said it did."

"You probably thought it," she grumbled. It happened more than she liked. Men couldn't handle a strong woman.

"I find your bossiness sexy."

"I am not bossy."

"Are you going to tell me how this trip is going to work?"

"Yes. But I'm sure you won't entirely listen."

"Gotta make it authentic, princess."

"Speaking of being nice, when you say princess, do so lovingly and not sarcastically."

"Yes, princess." He batted his lashes.

She snorted. "You look ridiculous."

"Shouldn't you have a pet name for me, too? My friends use Ash."

"That's for your friends. As lovers, we should use something different."

"Speaking of lovers, can you handle me touching you in public?"

"So long as you're not gross. I am not into PDA."

He blinked.

"Public displays of affection. So cheek pecks and hand holding good, tongue and hand up my shirt bad."

"Are you sure of that? Because I bet you'd enjoy it."

She wouldn't take that bet because she knew she would. "I agreed to be your fake partner, not your sex doll."

"Understood. Will you be okay with us sharing a room? My mom and sister don't have big places."

She held up a hand. "Hold on. I am not keen on guest rooms or couches. Not to mention that might put a little too much stress on our fake relationship. We should stay at a hotel. We can book one with a pair of queens so we each have our own bed."

"Are you worried about sharing with me, princess?"

"I can handle you if you get too frisky."

"Me? I was talking about you. We both know you want me."

"Do not," she huffed. A lie. She was all too aware of him across from her.

"Anyone looking at us will feel the sexual tension."

In this he might be correct. "And how do you propose we fix that?"

His slow grin warned her. "Copious amounts of orgasms beforehand."

It almost hurt to turn him down. "We don't have the time. We leave in the morning."

His turn to arch his brow. "Is that a challenge?"

The last time she tossed one, he made her come while fully dressed.

She smirked at him. "At least this time we have a bed." While usually bold, this was next level for Val. She preferred to dangle her lovers a little bit longer. Got them to buy her dinner and take her out. Made them pant and get to the point they begged.

With Asher, she was the one ready to beg.

Forget the fact they'd just met and that sleeping with him now would be awkward given she'd be around him for the next two weeks. She wanted him.

"I—" Whatever he might have said was interrupted as someone knocked on the door. "Hey, is Ash in there?"

"Wassup, Hammer?"

"I got a list of stuff I need you to grab while you're in the city. Loch has one, too. Oh, and Gary was saying something about tile for the bathroom."

Asher grimaced. "I'll be right there." He glanced at her. "Guess we'll have to delay that challenge."

She offered a coy smile. "What if it's only a one-time deal?"

"Then my loss. See you in the morning, princess. Sweet dreams of me." He winked and left.

Damn him if she didn't dream of him all night.

NINE

Asher escaped before he could change his mind and claim Val.

He wasn't ready to commit. Bad enough he'd somehow gotten embroiled in a plan to make her his fake wife. Maybe not fake for long. He had it bad for her.

It knotted his stomach while at the same time filled him with a tingling anticipation. Had he not been given the perfect excuse, he would have fucked her. Even as he knew he shouldn't. If they were fated, then sex would bind them for life. Hardly fair without her knowing the whole truth.

They were incompatible. He lived here, in the boonies. She was a city girl through and through.

Then again, fated mates were matched exactly because they were perfect, which meant she should be able to handle his Were side. But how to broach it given he couldn't admit the truth without having her oathbound first? Did he even dare? Half the time he wasn't even sure she liked him. His touch, yes. But Asher as a person? She mocked him at every turn.

He loved that about her. What if he was wrong, though? The last time he'd felt topsy-turvy it ended up with him having the piss beat out of him. The indecision led to him tossing and turning so much he fell out of the hammock twice before he resigned himself to sleeping on the porch.

"Ahem." Her cleared throat woke him the next day. Val stood over him, wearing pants unfortunately.

He rolled to his back. "Good morning, princess."

"Why are you outside?"

"Fresh air."

"Is this because I'm in your bed?"

"Don't tell me you're feeling guilty about taking it?" He rose on an elbow.

"No." She walked into the house, and after rising slowly, he followed. He showered and dressed before joining her at the kitchen counter where she ate a bowl of cereal—freshly made oatmeal with raisins—and drank some orange juice.

"Made something to stick to your gut." Poppy turned from the stove with another steaming bowl.

"Pass me the sugar." He seated himself and heaped many spoonfuls of brown sugar on top.

"Want any oatmeal with that?" Val's dry query.

"It's delicious," he said in between mouthfuls.

"I've packed a lunch and snacks for the trip." Poppy heaved an insulated cooler bag onto the counter.

Val's eyes widened, but Asher wasn't surprised.

"I hear we're doing the bachelorette in Edmonton?" Poppy shyly added.

"Yes. If all goes well, we'll have the penthouse of a hotel casino with four bedrooms, each with its own en suite and a huge living room with a view of the city."

"Sounds expensive."

"It is for most people. Not me. My cousin Cicily manages a casino resort on the outskirts of the city."

"How many cousins do you have?" Asher inquired. Because he'd lost count of her family members.

"Twenty-three. Maybe twenty-four if it turns out the baby is Uncle Giorgio's."

"Are you close to your family?"

Her nose wrinkled. "Depends on your idea of close. We're related. We see each other at the family functions I choose to attend. Which isn't many. My parents weren't exactly well regarded."

Don't ask why. Don't ask—

"Why?"

"Let's just say they were not upstanding citizens."

"Sorry to hear that."

"Why?" She regarded him with frankness. "There's no reason for you to give a shit. I don't. It is what it is. I survived their shitty parenting despite their best attempts."

"When do you want to leave?" he asked before he learned even more about her. Keeping his distance meant not getting too close. A good thing Val appeared willing to keep him at arm's length.

"Now."

"As you command, princess."

In short order they left with some back slapping and winks for him, Meadow talking a mile a minute and hugging Val fiercely.

He was in the passenger seat as Val drove like a psychopath escaping the end of the world.

The oh-shit bar got a workout. "Going a little fast?" An ironic thing to say given his own love of speed when he drove.

She pointed to the nav system with its estimated time of arrival. "Pretty sure I can shave at least an hour off that."

He arched a brow. "Only counts if we arrive alive."

"Are you scared of a woman driving?"

"More like scared of the moose that likes to suddenly get in front of cars and prove who's tougher."

"Hence why Cousin Vinny installed a push bar on the front."

He almost banged his head off the dash. The woman was nuts. And hot. A dangerous combination.

It took two hours into the trip—where he napped since he'd slept like shit—and then part one of Poppy's snacks for the road before he broached their upcoming visit with his mother and sister.

"We should probably get our stories straight," he said, trying not to flinch as she ate one-handed and took the turns at almost twice the posted speed limit.

"Stick to the truth as much as possible. It's what my Uncle Karlos would say. He's a lawyer. Backstory is easy. We met because of Meadow, fell madly in love, and got engaged almost right away."

A plausible scenario, except his family would know right away she wasn't his mate because she lacked his scent. "That might work if my family wasn't aware of my dislike of marriage."

"Why do you hate it?"

He shrugged. "Not hate it, more like not a fan. I think too many people get married for the wrong reasons."

"What's a right reason?"

It sounded dorky, but he said it anyway. "True love."

She snorted. "And how do you know if it's true or not?"

"You don't. Which is why I'd rather avoid it." A thing he'd said for years, and yet sitting beside Val he wanted something different. Wanted her.

"You're the one who said we needed to be a couple to visit. Which I still don't grasp. Is your cousin going to suddenly be less pissed because you're with someone?"

"Yes."

"That's dumb."

"More like complicated."

"Apparently. Is your family part of some other cult thing?"

His turn to utter a chuckle of amusement. "You might say so."

"How do we make it believable then? And if you say by fucking, I'm gonna dump your ass on the side of the road right now."

"No sex." Because sex would be the thing that

screwed them both. The lack of, though, gave him an idea. "Can you pretend you're religious?"

"I'm Italian Catholic. No need to pretend even if I don't believe or practice. Why?" She gave him a brief glance.

"Because good Catholic girls don't have sex before marriage."

Her laughter rang loud and bold. "You want me to pretend I'm a virgin?"

"It would explain why I was willing to get engaged. We could also then get separate rooms." He needed to keep the temptation far away if he was going to come out of this unscathed.

"Won't your family think you're playing me with the whole rapid engagement thing just to get in my pants?"

"They already think I'm a player."

"It has potential," she muttered. Then she glanced at him. "But it's also crazy. Who will believe I'm a virgin? Look at me. Almost thirty and hot as fuck."

"Unlucky in love thus far and determined to wait for Mr. Right."

"You?" She snickered. "I guess you're pretty enough it might be believable."

It better be, because the alternative was give in to the burning within and make her his mate.

TEN

AT THE HALFWAY POINT OF THEIR TRIP, VAL reluctantly allowed Asher to take a turn at the wheel. While he didn't drive as fast as her, he did travel decently over the speed limit, meaning they arrived in Edmonton by dinner. They only stopped twice because the coffee she chugged went right through her.

While they'd hashed out a plan of action—and exchanged personal details to make their fake engagement more real—they'd not counted on a convention messing with their decision to rent two rooms. The hotel overflowed with guests, many of them loud and already drunk. Her fault for not calling ahead. Or she could blame him. She'd not been herself since they met.

Asher grimaced. "Maybe we should go elsewhere."

"We'll only have to share for one night," she remarked. "Today is their last day."

"I guess." He didn't sound enthused, which annoyed her to no end.

First, the guy was hot and heavy with her, and now he did everything he could to stay far away. He'd not laid a single finger on her since their heavy make-out session. Hadn't even tried to touch her during the trip.

She'd kind of hoped—expected—him to fondle her and give her the aforementioned finger fuck. Now she had to hope the shower had a detachable head. Or would he turn back into the flirt once they got in the room? Because she'd swear he was still interested. She sure as hell remained in lust.

"Don't worry, gumdrop, I promise to not compromise your virtue."

"Gumdrop?"

"Because you're sweet and sticky?" she offered.

"You can't be serious."

"Picky, picky. You didn't hear me complain about your nickname for me."

"Mine has you pegged as royalty."

"Gumdrops are lovely to suck on." She offered him a guileless expression.

His Adam's apple bobbed before he said, "No."

"You're no fun. Don't worry, I'll think of something else." She winked. "Back to the room situation. You should thank me. We're getting the room at the favored family rate."

"If money is an issue, I can pay for two rooms elsewhere."

She snorted. "And offend my cousin? Stop arguing and bring in the bags."

She marched off, leaving him to tote them, because if he didn't, cousin Cicily would hear about it and report to the family. Then Val would have to deal with phone calls and messages about her shitty fiancé. As it was, she could just imagine the furor when the news got passed around she'd shown up with a man. At least it would shut up a few aunts who lamented that poor Valencia would be a spinster.

She probably would. Most men bored her. She glanced back at Asher easily toting her massive suitcase along with his own bag.

Asher didn't bore her. Not yet. But she'd only known him two days. He'd get annoying soon. Even if he didn't, she just had to remind herself he was a country boy. Even if they did keep hitting it off, it couldn't go anywhere because she wasn't moving away from the city. The suburbs were as far as she'd go.

The front counter was full of people. As if Val had to wait.

Cousin Cecily herself bellowed, "Valencia. Over here!"

The rather tall and broad woman waved at her, handsome of features, if sharp, her nose a bit hooked. Her aunt had never married and more than once offered a young Valencia to come live with her rather than her own parents. But that would have meant leaving Meadow behind in Calgary. Val preferred to visit with her BFF and get spoiled by her aunt.

She endured the giant hug and then the ogle as her aunt catalogued every inch of her.

"Too skinny," she declared before setting her gaze on Asher. She eyed him more intensely before smiling. "Too pretty."

The cad took Cicily's hand and kissed it. "I was about to say the same myself. I see good looks run in the family."

"Oh, he's a charmer," Cicily murmured. "Come. I'm afraid your room isn't my best. I only have one open because we kicked out its occupant. Thought he could slap the asses of my staff."

"Asshole," Val stated.

Whereas Asher flirted by saying, "Does this mean I can't give you a little love tap?"

"For you, I'll make an exception." Cicily actually tittered.

It almost made Val see red until she reminded herself that she didn't care.

As if sensing her annoyance, he slung an arm around her waist. "Maybe not while around my fiancée. She's the jealous type."

"Fiancée?" The groan almost rolled from Val as her aunt's face expressed shock. "She never said a word in her message. Just that she was bringing a friend." The last bit narrowed on Val with accusation.

"Surprise." A dry reply by Val.

"Where's the ring?" Cicily eyed her bare finger.

"One of the reasons we're here. Not much choice where I live, and well, I just couldn't wait to propose." Asher laid it on thick.

Cecily swallowed it. "I take it the family doesn't know."

"They will by morning I'm sure," Val muttered.

"Sooner." Cecily didn't even deny the fact she'd tattle. "Have you set a date? Chosen a location? You know we do weddings here."

"No date and, before you ask, the penthouse bachelorette party is for Meadow. And only

Meadow. I would never take away from her special day."

"Little Meadow getting married." Cecily shook her head. "Look at you both wanting to shackle yourself to one man."

"Only because she met the right guy," Asher crooned. "Since you asked, we'll probably get hitched soon. I can't wait to make Valencia mine."

A declaration that should have been repugnant. Instead, she shivered. Asher hugged her tighter, one arm for her, the other lugging their luggage. An admirable feat.

Her aunt stopped by the elevator and handed over two keycards. "These will get you in room 713 tonight, penthouse by three p.m. tomorrow. Room service is on me, so order whatever you like."

"Thanks."

"Don't thank me. You just gave me the best reward. Wait until everyone hears the news."

Only as the elevator doors closed did Val groan. "My phone is going to be ringing off the hook tonight."

"I thought you weren't close to your family."

"I'm not."

"Your aunt seems to really like you."

"She does. They all do. Doesn't mean I like them back." They'd all been witness to her childhood.

Offered to help her out. She'd refused. But the shame of it lingered. However, she didn't allow pride to stand in the way of the family deals. They got more offended when she did.

"Must be horrible to be so loved."

For some reason the teasing peeved. She jabbed him and moved out of his embrace. "You have no idea what you're talking about. So zip it, Sparkie."

"Sparkie? What kind of nickname is that?"

"Haven't you ever watched a Griswold movie?"

A moue of distaste twisted his lips. "Are you comparing me to Chevy Chase?"

"Well, you're both light haired and think you're funny." The elevator stopped, and the doors opened. She stepped out and didn't bother to check if he followed. No need. She sensed him as if he were on her radar.

The door to their room was at the far end by the stairs. Excellent. She opened it to find a decently sized space. Clean. Two beds. One bathroom. The view out the window was of the parking lot. About as big as his cabin, and yet as she turned around to see him shutting the door, it felt tiny.

He dropped the luggage on the first bed and stretched. "I don't know about you, but I could use a shower."

The remark had her imagining him naked and wet.

Mmm.

His expression smoldered, but he didn't make a move toward her. "Did you need to pee first?"

She needed something down there, but it wasn't what he suggested. "Go ahead. I'll be fine."

Only she wasn't. She kept eyeing that bathroom door. The unlocked door. He'd closed it but not engaged the lock. Would he protest if she joined him?

He'd not done anything to indicate he wanted her that close to him. Perhaps he was nervous about seeing his family.

When he finally emerged in a cloud of steam, a towel around his waist, she swallowed hard at the sight of his slick chest. Hairier than expected. Nice. Unexpected was the tattoo wrapping around his upper body, a stallion with a flowing mane.

He padded to his duffel bag. "I forgot clean clothes."

She forgot how to talk as she stared. The man was built like a god. Muscled. Lean. Lickable.

"Gotta pee." She ran into the bathroom, almost running a hand over his flesh as she passed. She turned on the water and splashed her face. Anything to simmer down the heat in her body.

She was just thinking about having her own shower when there was a knock at the door. Probably room service. Knowing her aunt, she'd sent up food or wine.

Wrong on both counts. As she emerged, it was in time to see Asher open the door to a woman who shrieked, "I'm so happy you're here!" Then the stranger threw herself at him.

Val almost snapped. Why? She didn't care who hugged Asher.

He'd admitted to being a manwhore. Was this the infamous cousin's wife that got him ostracized?

He turned, his arm around the young woman's shoulders, beaming. "Val, I'd like you to meet my little sister, Winnie. Winnie, say hello to my fiancée, Valencia."

"Fiancée!" More squealing ensued, along with some punching as his sister jabbed him in the ribs. "You jerk. You never told us you were seriously dating anyone."

"It was sudden," Val offered, her green-eyed monster tucking away now that it knew there was no reason for jealousy. Never mind the fact she shouldn't have given a damn at all.

"I can't believe it. I'm finally going to have a sister," Winnie declared then burst into tears.

ELEVEN

At the sight of the tears, Asher panicked. "Winnie, don't cry."

"It's happy tears," she blubbered. "I always wanted a sister."

"We're not married yet," Val interjected, looking as if she wanted to flee.

"I know. But you will. I know Asher. He wouldn't have brought you if it wasn't serious." Winnie wiped at the wet streaks. "Look at me. A hormonal mess."

"Still a big softy. You are looking awesome, sis."

Winnie beamed. "I do now. You should have seen me in the first trimester, puking all over. Poor Gordie. He was such a champ cleaning up after me."

"What are you doing here?" Asher asked, closing the door behind her.

"Dumb question. Do you know how long it's been since I saw you in person?" she complained.

A few years since he'd planned a trip to meet up with her in Calgary away from Rocco and his father. "We video chat each week."

"Not the same," she pouted before turning her attention to Val. "I'm so happy you found someone."

"More like she found me. She's best friends with Meadow, Rok's soon-to-be wife."

Winnie clapped her hands. "Oh, that's just perfect. Best friends marrying each other's best friends. All living together on the ranch."

Asher could see Val panicking, so he quickly stated, "We haven't decided yet where we'll stay. Val's more of a city girl."

"City as in Edmonton?" she asked hopefully.

"Calgary, actually," Val stated.

"Which is still closer than where you are now." Winnie's head bobbed. "I still can't believe you're engaged. I want to know everything."

"Not much to tell. It's been a whirlwind courtship. But how could I resist that puppy-dog face." Val neared them and pinched his cheeks as she cooed, "So adorable."

It was too much, but his sister grinned, eating it up. "Always was too cute for his own good. You can't imagine how excited I am to know he's found someone special."

He snared an arm around Val's waist, drawing her close. "She's special, all right." A drawled reply that saw him getting elbowed in the ribs.

"I am starved. We were just about to have dinner. Won't you join us?" Asher asked.

His sister laughed. "As if I'd say no to food. But I'm one step ahead, big brother. I left the baby at home with Gordie to come here. Mom's downstairs getting us a table."

"Mom is here, too?" He couldn't help the smile. It had been too long since he'd hugged her.

"As if she'd let me come by myself." Winnie rolled her eyes. "Ready to go?"

"Just give me a second to freshen up." Val hit her suitcase for some fresh clothes before she went into the bathroom.

Only when the fan turned on with the water did he lean close to whisper, "She doesn't know what we are."

"Isn't she your mate?"

"Yes." That part wasn't a lie. "I haven't claimed her yet."

"But you're engaged." His sister looked and sounded baffled.

"Long story short, she doesn't believe in sex

before marriage."

His sister laughed so hard she slapped hands to her boobs and squealed. "Stop joking, you're making me leak."

"Not that funny," he grumbled.

"What's not funny?" Val asked, emerging with her hair freshly brushed, her clear skin damp from washing. Her lashes were naturally dark and thick, but she'd added gloss to her lips. Cherry flavored.

Yum.

"My sister was just making fun of me for falling for you so quickly, princess."

"What can I say? The moment we met, I felt something for him. And it wasn't indigestion. It was lu-u-u-v, right, my big, hairy Wookie?" Val laid it on thick, and fuck him if he didn't like it.

But the name? "Wookie? What happened to babe?" He threw out a nickname he could live with.

As if Val would agree. "Everyone uses babe. Our spontaneous love deserves something better. More unique. More you."

"I like it," Winnie declared. "I always thought you sounded like one."

"Do not," he roared.

Val lifted a brow. "Don't you?"

Winnie chortled. "Oh, this is so much fun. Wait until mom meets her."

Unlike his excited sister—and amused fake fiancée—nervousness racked Asher. Would his mother see through their charade?

They headed downstairs to find his mom, who waved at them from the far end of the restaurant at a table tucked by the kitchen swinging door.

Val took one look and addressed the hostess. "That table won't do."

"I'm sorry, ma'am, that's all we had available at short notice."

Val arched a brow. "Are you sure about that?"

Something in her tone must have alerted the hostess. She stared at Val and muttered, "Oh dear. You're Ms. Ferrari's niece." The young woman looked quite flustered. "One moment please. It appears we've placed you at the wrong table. Anthony!" She snapped her fingers, drawing the attention of a waiter. "Move table forty-nine to the VIP room."

"What? Why?" Winnie looked confused.

Asher leaned close to murmur, "Val is the owner's niece."

"Oh. Cool." His sister had no problem getting upgraded. As for his mother, she looked bemused as she approached, but it quickly changed to joy upon seeing him.

"Asher." Mom reached for him and hugged him tight.

He hugged her back. Long and probably awkward for those watching. Too bad. When they did eventually separate, he kept an arm around her and turned his mom to see Val. "Mom, I'd like you to meet someone special to me. This is Valencia, my fiancée."

"Pleasure to meet you, ma'am." Val didn't curtsy but did bob her head.

"Don't ma'am me. You're engaged. Call me mom." That quickly, his mom threw herself at Val, who had a look of panic in her eyes at the hug. "Another daughter. What a lovely surprise. And soon more grandbabies. I'm so blessed."

As his mom and sister followed their waiter to the new table, Asher leaned close enough to whisper, "Regretting your offer yet?"

She cast him a grin over her shoulder. "How many babies we having, Wookie? Two, three, four so we can form our own hockey team?"

His mom and sister beamed that whole meal and got along famously with Val. They found it highly entertaining the sarcastic way she treated him.

When Val excused herself to use the restroom, his mother declared, "I like her a lot, Ashie. She's just the kind of strong woman you need in your life. Although I am surprised to hear she's religious. She doesn't seem the type."

No, she didn't, with her swaying hips and bold stare.

"She's worth the wait," Asher assured, even as his blue balls did not agree.

"Don't wait too long. You wouldn't want the mating instinct to turn into a fever," his mother warned.

The mating fever being a supposed affliction that hit those who didn't give in to the passion and claim their chosen mate.

"Don't worry about me, Mom." He expected to feel bad about the lying, only what came out of his mouth wasn't exactly false. He did want Val. He could see them having a future. Fuck, since the topic had first come up, he'd changed his mind. He could now even see them with kids. A boy and a girl at the very least, the girl as feisty as her mother.

"Uh-oh." His mother stiffened, and Asher didn't have to turn to look. He sensed the arrival of another Were. Recognized the irritating drawl of Rocco, who, of course, had to stop by their table with a woman, not his wife, on his arm.

"So much for this place being VIP," he muttered. He hated the brief expression of fear on his mother's and sister's faces as the Alpha's son stopped by their table.

Forget polite niceties. The fucker snapped,

"Well, well, look who came home. Without permission. Have you forgotten what you were told?"

Winnie jumped to his rescue. "Asher's found his mate. They're engaged to be married."

"Really?" Rocco drawled. "I don't see her. Is she invisible?"

"She's right here." Val appeared behind the man and had a cold haughty glare for Rocco. Asher stood quickly, and she tucked herself into his side. "Sorry, Wookie, I got delayed by a cousin on my way back."

Rocco scowled at Val. "Who are you?"

"None of your business." Ice frosted her words.

As if Rocco would back down. "My city. My business."

"Excuse me? Someone has a high opinion of himself." Val's spine turned rigid. "Asher, who is this rude buffoon interrupting our lovely dinner?"

"Rocco Durante."

"Ah, the infamous cousin."

The guy smirked. "I see you've heard of me."

"I wouldn't be so smug about it." Val eyed him up and down before curling her lip. "I can see why you didn't keep in touch. I've no use for bottom feeders either, even when they are family."

"You can't talk to me like that, bitch," Rocco snapped.

To which Asher replied, very quietly, "Watch your tone around my fiancée."

Winnie jumped in. "Isn't this amazing? My brother engaged. It was love at first sight."

Rocco's nostrils flared. "Bullshit. Wait until my father hears you lied your way back into town."

Before Asher could tell Rocco to go fuck himself, Val stepped in front of him. "Listen here, little man—and I mean *little*—I don't like your tone or your implication. Asher is my fiancé. It might have been a rushed courtship but only because we decided there was no point in wasting time. And you are now interrupting my dinner with my lovely new mother and sister-in-law."

"I will interrupt if I damned well like because I run this fucking city." Rocco drew himself tall. Bristling. The aggression just below the surface.

Val got even taller it seemed as she stared him down. "No, you don't." Val lifted her hand and snapped her fingers.

As if called, a hotel guard dressed in a dark uniform appeared. "Is this person bothering you?"

"He is. Could you have him removed please?" Val asked, paying the reddening Rocco no mind.

"At once, ma'am." The guard turned to Rocco. "Sir, it's time to go."

As if Rocco would go quietly. "Like fuck I'm

going."

"It's not a debate, sir. Either leave now or I will be forced to physically remove you."

"Fuck you."

The guard went to grab Rocco, who shifted out of reach.

"Don't you fucking touch me. I demand to speak to a manager."

Val appeared amused. "Go ahead. Tell my aunt about how you insulted her favorite niece."

Rocco scowled. "This isn't over."

"Didn't figure it would be," Asher muttered. He'd hoped to avoid Rocco entirely, but now that the man felt insulted...

A good thing they wouldn't be staying long. The christening was tomorrow. They could be on the road by the next morning, or even that same night if things got too tense.

Rocco stalked out, and it might have been the end of their evening if Val hadn't brightly announced, "Who's in the mood for dessert? I hear the chef makes a mean mousse."

It also involved wine, with even Winnie having a glass since she'd pumped some milk for the baby already. His mom got quite giggly, and he got to see a softer side to Val, which included smiles aimed at him and rich laughter.

When they finally parted, with hugs and promises to see each other the next day, he placed an arm around Val's tipsy frame to guide her to their room.

"I can walk fine," she declared, bouncing off the edge of the elevator door.

"I see that."

When the elevator lurched into motion, she swayed, and he steadied her. To his surprise, she leaned into his embrace.

"I think that went well," she murmured.

"My family liked you."

"They weren't awful." She glanced up at him. "I don't like lying to them."

"Me either." But the alternatives were few. Walk away from Val and his family or claim his mate and then somehow get her oathbound so he could reveal his secret. Doable, but then what? City girl and country boy. How would they make it work?

It was his conscience that reminded, *You didn't always live in the boonies.* Once upon a time, he liked living in the midst of it all.

The elevator opened, and he kept his hand in the middle of Val's back as she went up the hall. About to follow her into the room, Asher paused upon seeing movement behind the fogged window of the door to the stairwell.

Could be a patron, or Rocco planning another ambush.

"Let's get you to bed," he said, first aiming Val at the bathroom. When she emerged, he handed her a T-shirt of his rather than rummage through her things.

She eyed it then him. "That's not mine."

"Wear it. I have a feeling we might get a morning visitor."

Her lip curled. "Your nasty cousin again?"

"Doubtful. He's more the ambush-in-the-shadows type. But my sister might just decide we need coffee and donuts."

"And your shirt helps make it look real. Got it." She began to pull off her top.

Oh fuck. He whirled before he saw too much flesh.

"I'm a little restless. I'm going to take a walk before bed."

"Will you be safe by yourself?"

Safer out there than in here with her, where he might do the inconceivable. "I'll be fine. Go to bed. I'll be back soon."

He fled before she hammered at his resolve. He leaned against the hotel room door for a second before eyeing the stairwell.

Probably nothing. Just in case, though, he didn't

want to expose Val to possible violence. Not to mention, he could use something to burn off some steam. He almost hoped he'd find Rocco when he opened the door.

Instead, he groaned as the waiting Kit said, "Glad you changed your mind."

The red-headed man sat on the steps, casual like.

"How long have you been skulking here?" Asher grumbled.

"Long enough to know you saw Rocco Durante."

"I did. And FYI, he's still an asshole."

"Being an asshole isn't enough to get him sanctioned. We need more."

Asher raked a hand through his hair. "More like what?"

"Evidence of a crime. Breaking of Were rules." The Lykosium were very much about toeing the straight and narrow laws of humans. The fewer reasons they had to get arrested and placed under scrutiny, the better.

"Still don't see how I'm supposed to help. Our meeting didn't go well."

"I'm sure you'll figure something out."

"What if I don't want to get involved?"

Kit stood and said flatly, "Is that really the answer you want me to take back to the Lykosium?"

"No." Spoken with a slight sulk.

"Report back when you find something."

"How?"

"I'm in your contacts."

Asher didn't ask how he'd managed that, given his phone had remained in his pocket the whole evening. "What if I don't find anything?"

"We both know that's not likely. Nor advisable. I hear you're engaged to a human." Kit glanced past him to the hall door.

"Val knows nothing about us," he hastened to say.

"Yet. Remember the rules," Kit warned. "Your Alpha got lucky with his mate."

"I know."

Rok almost lost Meadow because she found out about the Were secret before being oathbound.

"I'll be waiting to hear from you." The man melted into the shadows lacing the stairs, going up, not down.

Freaky fucker. Why did he not have a scent?

Asher waited a moment longer before returning to the hotel room and a slightly snoring Val.

He stared at her a moment. To claim or not to claim. He was beginning to wonder if that was even a question.

TWELVE

Val woke and stretched. Only as she rolled in the unfamiliar bed did she remember where she was—and with who.

Asher.

A man who fired every single one of her senses. No wonder when she got drunk she practically begged him to screw her. But did he take advantage? No! He chose to be a perfect fucking gentleman and walk away.

He probably thinks I'm a slut.

She revised that thought because a woman enjoying sex didn't make her anything but healthy and normal. However, twice now he'd rejected her. She really needed to stop fantasizing about him because he'd obviously lost interest.

Asher lay sprawled in the bed across from her,

blankets kicked off, wearing only a pair of shorts. Nothing else.

Damn that was a lot of nice flesh to ogle. Muscled. Tanned working-man style, the delineation showing around his upper arms and neck.

Just her luck, he caught her staring and offered a lazy smile. "Morning, princess."

"Hey, Wookie."

He groaned. "Can't you think of something better?"

"You've hated every suggestion thus far."

"I'm good with babe. Even honey."

"Boring. What about snookums?"

"No one will ever believe you're the type to use that."

"Good point."

"Stud, though..."

She snorted. "That remains to be seen."

"Is that a complaint?"

"Yes. Why must you always be a gentleman?" With that rebuke she stomped to the bathroom. When she reemerged, he remained undressed, chest bared and showing a bit of hair arrowing down into a vee at his waist, hands laced behind his head, watching the weather network of all things.

"Supposed to rain hard the next few days," he observed.

She frowned. "I told Meadow to be here tomorrow with the girls for the bachelorette. Will it be safe to drive? How will they even get here? The truck is broken."

"Gary keeps an old Buick sedan in the garage. Thing is in mint condition and built like a tank. It can handle it."

"Says you."

"Rok won't let anything happen to her."

"Hmph." It stung a bit that someone else would be the person Meadow relied on. While busier these days with her job, Val liked being the one Meadow turned to.

"Don't be such a fussy pants. She will be fine. And so will you, my control freak of a princess."

"Says the man not planning the most epic party."

"Says who? You're not the only one planning a sendoff."

"Let me guess, strippers and beers."

His wide grin held not a hint of repentance as he drawled, "You forgot shenanigans. Or have you not watched *The Hangover*?"

"I saw the first one. It was enough."

"Would you feel better if I said I never drink?"

"Why not?" she asked. It hadn't occurred to her he'd eschewed the wine the night before. As a matter of fact, she'd yet to see him imbibe. At the same time, they'd met only days ago, hardly enough time to know all his bad habits.

"I swore off hooch and dope after it got me into trouble when I was younger. The shit made me stupid. I vowed to never touch it again."

"Do you miss it?"

"Nah. Turns out I don't need booze to have a good time. And being the sober one means there's no embarrassing videos of me doing the macarena."

Her lips curved. "I wish I could say the same." A certain wedding video of a cousin had her not only jiving to the popular dance but doing the conga.

"You still okay with going to see the baby before the christening? You can bail if you want."

"A good fiancée wouldn't miss it. Besides, I like your family." A surprise she accidentally admitted. "They are pretty awesome, and you are obviously close, which makes it even stranger that you'd give a damn what a piece of shit says."

"That piece of shit has a lot of friends."

"So do you."

He arched a brow. "Are you suggesting I bring them to town and beat Rocco and his buddies to a pulp?"

"That's one solution."

The corner of his mouth quirked. "Except I'm about making love, not war."

"Can't believe you'd rather fake an engagement," she said with a shake of her head.

"I really appreciate what you're doing."

"Whatever." She waved away the thanks. "I can't believe he's such a petty dick that he's still holding a grudge ten years later. Gotta say, his wife looked younger than expected."

"That wasn't his wife."

Her mouth rounded. "Oh. What an even bigger jerk then. He's cheating on her, and yet he's still being an asshole to you?"

"Yeah."

"Maybe someone should tell his wife."

At that, he sighed. "It wouldn't do anything. I'm sure she already knows."

"I'd castrate a man who cheated on me."

"Why would anyone step out on you? You're perfect." His eyes widened as if he'd not meant to say the last part. "I should shower."

He practically ran to hide in the bathroom, and she stared pensively at the door. He liked her. So why hadn't he touched her since that passionate embrace when she'd given him a tow?

By the time he was ready, they had to leave if they were going to have time to buy some gifts. They grabbed breakfast from a coffee shop to eat before hitting a few stores. Then it was time to be social.

His sister lived in a townhouse that required parking farther away and walking back. Hand in hand. Asher caught her looking down at their clasped fingers. Casual and yet enjoyable.

"What's wrong?" he asked.

"I've never held hands with a guy before."

"Why not?"

"I don't know." The honest reply. But she had a good guess it had to do with her independent nature. Most men treated her as boss bitch, practically untouchable, and she encouraged it. Asher saw the assertiveness and respected it while treating her as a woman. It meant he opened doors for her. Held out chairs and even stood until she was seated. He held hands and, when the walkway narrowed, allowed her to go ahead.

She enjoyed it more than expected.

The door whipped open before they could knock, and Winnie squealed loud enough the whole neighborhood heard. "Uncle Ashie and Auntie Val are here!"

Auntie Val? It never occurred to her this charade would have Asher's sister welcoming her so readily into her family.

"Hold on a second. I forgot the gifts." Asher bolted back for the SUV.

Luckily, she'd managed to talk him out of the

giant stuffed teddy and the drum set but did approve of the lamp that projected the stars on the ceiling and provided white noise. He only raised his brows as she bought a few ridiculously girly outfits.

He returned bearing gifts, and Winnie shook her head. "You do realize having you here was present enough."

"If I want to spoil my niece, I shall! Where is she? Uncle Ash needs to hold her," he declared.

Entering the home meant being bombarded the baby stuff. Swing in the living room, along with something Winnie called a bouncy seat. A baby monitor on the kitchen counter showed a man leaning over a crib, lifting a small bundle.

The baby was cute with fine lashes and a rosebud mouth. But the thing that truly made her ovaries ache?

Seeing Asher holding the baby, his expression soft, his grip sure. What kind of father would he make? She'd often wondered what type of mother she'd be. Hopefully not as negligent as her own who, along with her father, was too busy with her own life and vices to pay attention to a child. Her father loved gambling. Mother, it was pills.

They'd died in a car accident during her college years. She still remembered standing by their graves, wishing she could cry but just feeling relief.

"Your turn, Auntie Princess," Asher declared, holding out the baby.

Val offered an evil eye to his grin but gingerly took the child dressed in a pink sleeper. So tiny, she peered at Val with vivid blue eyes, her shock of dark hair almost long enough to put in a tiny bow.

To her surprise Asher put an arm around her and murmured, "Didn't think you could look any sexier."

The remark surprised her, and that was the picture Winnie managed to grab. A picture that she kept peeking at on her phone after Winnie texted it. Seeing her, Asher, and that baby had her suddenly longing for something she never knew she wanted, but now might need.

A family of her own.

THIRTEEN

Seeing Val holding his niece twisted something in Asher. Or reinforced what he'd known from the moment they met.

She's my mate.

Apparently, it didn't matter they were opposites. The more time he spent with her, the harder it became to hold back the passion simmering under his skin. Sleeping in the same room with her, being so close, he'd never survive. The best he could at this point was take things slow. Ease Val into the idea they were meant for each other. Then reveal his secret and have her swear the Oath.

But what if she refused? Or shot him with her little gun?

Better he die than she find out his secret and not be bound because the consequence for her would be dire. The knowledge of the Were existence had to be protected at all costs. Even if it meant taking a life.

Lunch was a boisterous affair. The baby was passed around, though she slept for most of it. Mom arrived to lend a hand, not that Winnie needed it. Her husband had taken advantage of the paternity option offered by his work. A man unafraid to be a father and partner to his mate. Asher liked the fellow, especially when Gordie exclaimed, "Thank fuck there's another guy around. Maybe now I won't always be outvoted." To which the women laughed.

The christening, scheduled for that afternoon, would happen in a church. Gordie might be Were, but he came from a family and Pack with strong Protestant ties.

To Asher's surprise, it was Val who grimaced as they entered the holy place. "This brings back unpleasant memories of Sunday mornings."

"Parents were religious?" he asked.

"Nope. But my grandparents were, and they insisted on bringing me every Sunday lest my parents' heathen natures corrupt me. I didn't mind as a kid, but the teenage years when I liked sleeping in were rough."

"I can't see you as a good Catholic girl."

"Only because I haven't put on my plaid skirt

and white blouse." She winked, the visual she presented definitely a sin.

Definitely something he wanted to see.

There were quite a few people inside. Gordie's family was on the left, not many given the Alpha in these parts didn't want too many outside Weres in his town. People there for Winnie, meaning the Pack, took the spots on the right.

To anyone casually glancing in, they wouldn't have known they observed two different Packs of Were. Being Canadian, both sides showed a diversity of appearance. Big, small. Skin of varying shades. Loud, quiet. But ignore the outward aspects, along with the artificial scents, and he could smell the difference. Feel it. Just like they probably noted his scent, which had shifted when Rok became Alpha of their newly formed Pack. Nova once joked that it was the equivalent of esoteric pissing to leave an identifiable mark.

Scent meant everything in the Were world, and everyone there knew Val didn't carry his. Hopefully that wouldn't cause issue. Too many eyes tracked his passage as he headed up the aisle to the reserved pew at the front. He took a spot beside his mom with Val on the other side of him. His keen hearing meant he caught some of the whispers at his back.

"Got a lot of nerve coming back after what he did."

"Engaged to a human. What a waste."

"Does Rocco know?"

Yeah, the fucker knew, and Asher doubted Rocco would let his return slide quietly. He pegged his arrival as a prickling sensation on his nape, but he didn't turn.

The baptism went well, with the baby yodeling her displeasure at being dipped in the basin. The reception afterwards, held in the basement, went off without a hitch. Asher made sure to steer clear of Rocco and Bruce, who'd yet to say anything to him. Just in case, Asher did make a show of touching Val more often than necessary, not just to reinforce the fact they were together but because he couldn't help himself.

In return, she smiled at him often and tended to lean into him, her arm snaking around his waist when new people would approach to say hello. More people than expected, to his surprise.

He'd prepared himself to be a pariah, and for them to steer clear, but while a few cast nervous glances at the ruling Durantes, most appeared genuinely happy to see him. It was when Val left to use the ladies' room that the one person he could have done without approached.

"Hi, Asher." Melinda's soft murmur had him clenching his jaw before turning.

He'd seen her in the church, looking as beautiful as ever. A beauty that left him cold. Unlike the days of his dumb youth, there was no rush of excitement upon seeing her. No pang of longing. Just annoyance.

"What do you want?" he curtly asked.

She appeared taken aback but didn't retreat. "It's good to see you."

"Is it?" He arched a brow and didn't smile.

"You're still mad." Her lower lip jutted.

"What did you expect?"

"I don't know. But I'm glad you're here so I can tell you that I'm sorry for what happened all those years ago. I wish I could go back and change things."

"You're not the only one who would do things differently."

She misunderstood his words. "In retrospect, I should have seen you were the better choice."

"Choice? You used me as your free fuck before marriage."

His words were crude enough anger flared, but Melinda quickly recovered. "Because I really liked you. I've thought about that time so much since then. I wish I'd been braver. That I could have stood up to Rocco and been with you. But I was scared."

He snorted. "That's bullshit, and you know it. You wanted the power he offered."

She moistened her lower lip, a thing that used to drive him wild but he now saw as contrived. "I was wrong. I see that now."

"And yet you're still married to him."

"Because I'm afraid. I'm not big and strong like you." She tried soft flattery.

It failed to move him. "Your husband is your problem. Not mine."

"You loved me once."

"And had it stomped on. Literally. As you can see, I've moved on."

Her lip curled. "With a human."

"She's my mate."

"And yet she doesn't bear your scent," Melinda tartly pointed out.

"Because she has morals." All he said and yet Melinda recoiled before she spat, "We both know she's not right for you."

"That's where you're wrong. Excuse me." He took leave of Melinda upon seeing Val return, looking for him.

For a second, her expression softened as their gazes locked then hardened as she glanced past him. Jealousy shone in her sparking eyes. As if Melinda, or any woman for that matter, could hold a candle to her.

He moved in her direction, only to have her lift her chin, whirl, and stalk off. It took him a moment to catch up to her outside the church's reception area.

"What's wrong, princess? The tiny sandwiches not up to your standards?"

"I need some air."

"You're pissed about something."

"Am not."

"You are. Dare I say even jealous?"

She whipped around and jabbed him in the chest. "Am not."

"You are, and might I say, it's rather hot?"

She uttered a disparaging noise. "Oh please. Stop pretending you like me. I see now why you haven't made a move since we left on this trip. You still have a thing for her."

"Who?"

"Melinda. Your cousin's wife."

He chuckled loudly. "You couldn't be more wrong if you tried."

"Oh, then explain why you went from trying to seduce me to only flirting when we have an audience."

He stepped closer. "Because if I kiss you, I'm

going to want to make love to you. And once we do, there's no turning back. We'll be together for life."

At that statement, her breath halted and then emerged in laughter. "You seriously have the biggest ego I've ever met."

"That's not the biggest thing about me," he teased.

She hit him. "Stop it."

"Stop what?"

"Pretending you're hot for me."

"It's not a pretense, princess. I have it bad for you. I'm also serious when I say having sex will change things between us."

"Only if you're bad at it and I have to avoid you until after Meadow's wedding."

His jaw dropped before he adopted a rueful grin. "I promise, it won't be bad."

"Guess I'll never know."

She went to march past him, but he grabbed her by the arm and whirled her into his chest. Then he kissed her. Kissed her with all the pent-up passion simmering within. Left her panting, wet, needing.

In the wrong place, wrong time, seeing as how someone cleared their throat loudly.

"What?" he snapped without turning his head.

"Your sister is looking for you," was Gordie's

amused reply. "We were about to leave. Baby's had enough excitement for the day."

"Coming," he growled, looking at Val. Her lips were swollen from his embrace, her eyes heavy lidded with passion.

Mine.

Fuck it. He was done fighting it. The two of them were meant to be.

Tonight. Once he got her back to that hotel, it was time to give in to the passion simmering under his skin, to claim her. Once Rok arrived with Meadow and they convinced Val to take the oath, he could admit his secret.

It was a great plan that had him anxious with anticipation, which might be why he insisted they run errands then have dinner before heading back to their hotel as night settled in.

They were waylaid along the way.

FOURTEEN

Ever since the kiss that was rudely interrupted, Val had been in a state of anticipation. A good thing Asher got them out of the church. Her wet panties had her feeling self-conscious. It didn't help that she'd have sworn a bunch of his family kept looking at her and smirking as if they knew. Impossible, yet she was glad to escape.

Only instead of going back to the hotel to do something about the longing, he had them grabbing things from his list. Then, he insisted on dinner. The delay only made her lust worse, because he kept touching her.

A hand to the middle of her back.

His fingers lacing with hers.

Feeding her parts of his dinner from his fork and spoon.

By the time he said a husky, "Ready to go to bed?" she really debated finding a dark alley and jumping him.

She insisted he drive, too distracted to focus on the road. And then, because he seemed a little too in control, she put her hand on his thigh as he drove. Slid it up and down his leg until he growled, "Keep doing that and our first time will be on the hood of your SUV."

"You do know the back seats fold flat and we've got more than eight feet of room, right?"

"I'll remember that for the trip back to the ranch. But today, we will make it to a bed. I haven't tortured myself this long to get a ticket for indecent exposure."

He broke speed limits getting them to the hotel, which sat on the outskirts of the city. He exited the highway and pulled to a stop behind a pickup truck halted at a red light.

The light turned green, and instead of taking off, the driver of the red truck got out.

Val frowned. "What's he doing?"

Asher put the SUV in park. "It's one of my cousin's friends. Stay in the car. Better yet, get to the hotel where there's people. They won't dare touch you in public."

"You can't be serious? I am not leaving you."

"Too late," he muttered.

A glance behind showed them hemmed in by another truck. Rocco emerged from it.

"You've got to be fucking kidding me," she muttered. "What are they planning to do?"

"Probably slap me around a bit and make some threats."

She blinked at him. "That is not okay."

"I can handle a few punches, and I don't really give a fuck what they say."

"Well, I care," she huffed.

"You're cute when you're worried." He cupped the back of her head and planted a brief kiss on her lips. "Lock the doors once I get out."

Before she could react, Asher spilled out of the SUV, one man against many. Perhaps it wouldn't come down to a fight.

They moved off far enough she could only hear the murmur of voices. Rocco's expression held a smugness she itched to slap, whereas his three thug friends scowled and tried to look intimidating.

The guy at Asher's back suddenly grabbed him in a bear hug. Rocco swung. Val hopped from her SUV and fired her gun in the air.

The sudden silence brought all eyes on her. She aimed her gun at Rocco. "Back away from my man."

"Princess, get back in the car. I got this," Asher declared.

"Listen to the cheating motherfucker and put the toy away—"

"Are you hard of hearing, asshole?" She fired again, shearing Rocco's ridiculous cowlick of hair.

Rocco's eyes widened. "You fucking cunt!"

"I'd watch the name calling, or next time I will aim for a smaller target." Her gaze dipped to a spot below his waist, and she smirked.

Finally, the dipshit looked worried. "You wouldn't dare."

"Actually, I would."

"Shoot me and I'll have you arrested," Rocco blustered.

"If I shoot you, I'll tell my uncle on the force that you carjacked us and it was self-defense. Guess who he'll believe?" Her smile widened, and she turned her attention to the guy holding Asher. "Let my fiancé go." When he glanced to Rocco instead of obeying, she barked, "Now."

The fellow stepped back and lifted his hands. "Fine. No need to PMS about it."

"I should shoot you just for being a misogynistic asshole," she muttered, her trigger finger itching to pull.

"She's nuts," someone exclaimed.

"Yes, she is. Now you see why I love her." Her fake fiancé grinned.

"Get back in your trucks before I decide to see which one of you can scream loudest when shot."

The trio of thugs scattered, but Rocco's lip lifted. "This isn't over."

"Are you really going to threaten me? My grand-mother used to say there's only one way to make sure my enemies never come back to haunt me. Now mind, she preferred poison masked as natural causes, but I can't cook. I do, however, have excellent aim." The gun pointed at Rocco's head.

"You'll pay for this," Rocco growled, the words low and guttural.

She blamed the falling twilight for the odd glint in Rocco's eyes.

The trucks and their thugs took off, tires spitting gravel. She waited for Asher to say something.

To bitch about being emasculated.

To freak out because she'd threatened to kill.

She should have known he'd be different.

The guy vaulted the hood of her car, dragged her into his arms, and kissed her!

FIFTEEN

Asher had never seen anything more terrifying or sexy than Val protecting his ass. Although he would have acted if she hadn't. He'd been about to bust out of Larry's grip when Val emerged from the SUV, showing unimaginable bravery.

And stupidity.

He ceased the kiss to harangue her. "You idiot! What were you thinking, putting yourself in danger like that?"

She arched a brow. "Is that how you say thank you?"

"Rocco and his friends aren't easily cowed. That could have ended very badly."

The corner of her mouth quirked. "It could have. For them. I am an excellent shot."

"With limited bullets."

"Do you really think this is my only gun?"

A wave of emotion hit him. He dropped to a knee on the spot and held her hand as he offered a fervent, "Valencia, you are the most perfect woman I've ever met. Marry me."

She laughed. "You're being silly."

"And if I wasn't? You are incredible."

The praise brought a blush to her cheeks. "Stop fooling around and get back in the car."

"So that's a no?" He gave her a look that had dropped countless panties.

With Val, he got laughter. "No, I am not marrying you, but I might let you get to second base if you're good. Third if you get us there without being stopped by anyone else."

The promise had him practically running to get back behind the wheel. Val seated herself beside him, and he just about killed them when her hand skipped his thigh and cupped his groin.

Holy fuck. This was going to happen.

He parked in front of the hotel and threw her keys at the valet, along with a twenty. Then shifted impatiently as Val swiped her room key so that the poor guy knew who the SUV belonged to.

The hotel was busy this time of night with the gamblers having descended in droves to spend their paychecks. He kept a hand in the middle of her back, guiding her toward the elevator. They were waylaid by Aunt Cecily, who planted herself in their path.

"There you are. You've been gone all day."

"Baby shower for his sister," Val explained.

"A baby, eh?" Cecily eyed them both and smiled. "I wouldn't mind a great-niece or nephew to spoil. With your genes, you'd make a cute one."

"How about one of each?" Asher offered, sliding his arm around Val's waist.

Cecily beamed. "That would be perfect."

"Was there something you needed to talk to me about?" Val asked.

"Just thought I'd let you know in person that the penthouse is ready for you and I had your things moved from your room."

"Thank you!" Val gave her aunt a one-armed hug. "If you don't mind, Asher and I are tired. Long day."

"Sure, it was," Cecily snorted with a knowing smirk. "See you tomorrow."

As they piled into the elevator, Asher chuckled. "She totally knows what we're going to do."

"Ya think?" Val grimaced. "Aunt Cecily's always been the free spirited one. She was the one who bought me a vibrator and told me I didn't need a man for sex."

"As a man, I'd like to disagree."

Her smile hit him hard as she purred, "Guess you'll have to prove it."

"Challenge accepted, princess." He pulled her into his arms and kissed her, the passion he'd been holding in threatening to spill over. As they arrived at the top floor and managed to swipe the key card while still groping and kissing, he retained enough wits to stop and ask, "Are you sure you want to do this? Because I'm warning you now, you will be stuck with me forever."

"Only if you're good," she teased, drawing him back for another kiss.

Entering the penthouse suite, he had little time to admire the lavish décor. She dragged him into the nearest bedroom and shoved him onto the bed.

He might have protested, only she began to strip, removing her clothes with little finesse. She wasn't drunk this time, which meant he could admire without guilt. So much to admire, from the indent of her waist to her flaring hips to the heft of her breasts.

Despite burning with desire, he managed a drawled, "Do me next."

Her fingers were deft as she unbuttoned his shirt and undid his pants. He helped her to tug off his slacks before he shrugged off his top.

Naked, they came together in a meld of heated

flesh that had him almost mindless. The bed, king sized and covered in a smooth duvet, provided a plush backdrop for her body, which he covered with his. Skin-to-skin, their mouths meshed, a tangle of erotic kisses involving much tongue. He tried to be careful and hold his weight off of her, but she kept grabbing him and pulling him down, her legs wrapping around him to lock him in place.

"I'm too heavy," he protested into her mouth.

"I'm not going to break," she growled in reply.

Still, he held back, not wanting to scare her with his untamed passion. This first time would be quick enough as it was without him losing control. But did she appreciate the thin leash he had on himself?

Nope. She was determined to make him come undone.

She shoved at him and purred an order. "Get on your back."

"Not yet. I'm hungry." And by hungry he meant for a taste of her breasts. He trailed kisses down her neck to the valley between them. He cupped their rounded weight, pushing them together for easy teasing. He pulled the bud taut and gave it a suck. She reacted with a moan and full-body shiver.

He kept sucking and playing, his leg wedged between hers, pressing against the heated core of her sex. Her wetness and scent drove him wild. He wanted to make her come. Wanted to feel her cream against his mouth.

Before he could give her a tongue-lashing, she shoved at him and once more demanded, "Get on your back!"

"Fine," he huffed in resignation. Not really that upset because the thought of her touching him...

Hmm. Hopefully he didn't embarrass himself.

She sat up and spent a second staring at his body. She traced a line down his chest, causing him to shiver and swallow hard, especially when she got to his groin. He lay still, waiting for her next move, tense with anticipation, his cock, rigid with arousal, jutting upward.

He reached to touch her, and she allowed it before saying huskily, "Hands behind your head. No touching while I play."

"That seems wildly unfair. Why should you get all the fun?" He pouted.

She laughed. "Don't worry. You're not done with me yet." With that said, she straddled his waist, her honey-slick core resting on his muscled stomach. She leaned forward and slid her lips across his, licking the seam of his mouth, nipping his bottom lip.

He reached out and cupped her ass.

"I said hands behind your head."

"You're just being cruel," he moaned.

"Deal with it." Her lips traced the edge of his jaw, nipping it lightly with her teeth.

He trembled and burned, but he didn't budge.

"That's my good Wookie." She smiled against his skin as she trailed a sensuous path down his neck, giving the spot where his pulse ticked a hard suck.

But it was when she bit him that his body went stiff under hers, and it was all he could do not to howl.

She continued to suck as she stroked his chest, dragging her nails over his nipples then tweaking them when they puckered in response. She slid farther down. Her wetness hit his cock, and he couldn't help a tiny buck of his hips.

"Bad Wookie. Stay still or I won't do this to your cock." She took one of his nipples into her mouth and sucked.

Fuck. Me.

He couldn't help but tremble and grab at the sheets as she toyed with him. Eventually, he had to gasp, "Enough. I need to touch you."

"Need?" she teased. "I have something that you can play with."

It shocked him when she repositioned herself so that her sex hovered over his mouth. She straddled him backwards, her mouth blowing warmly on his dick.

Oh, hell yeah. He grabbed her thighs and tugged her down for a taste, only to find himself distracted as her lips brushed the tip of his cock. She licked the swollen head of his dick before she slid her lips down his thick length. Then up again. Down. Up.

At least she lowered herself enough he could lick, too. He devoured the honeyed core of her, his tongue delving between her nether lips, tasting, flicking.

While he feasted, she sucked and bobbed. As if that weren't enough, she cupped his balls and kneaded until they pulled taut.

He hummed as he teased her clit. Felt her clench as he managed to wedge two fingers in her while working that swollen button.

He brought her to the edge and then tilted her over it, her orgasm a ripple that had her mouth clamping down tight on him.

His hips jerked, and he came, too.

And she took his cream. Swallowed it like he savored her. She sucked him dry as he kept licking. Tasting her. Wanting even more.

He wanted to sink his cock into her and imprint her with his flesh. The very thought had him hardening already.

She chuckled against his flesh. "All ready for round two?"

Hell yeah, he was. He flipped them around and spent a second admiring her. Her face flushed with passion, her eyelids half open and sensuous. Her legs were parted and waiting for him to fuck her.

Which was when they heard laughter.

Feminine laughter, and one grumpy male saying, "Where's Asher?"

SIXTEEN

Nothing like having sudden visitors while still basking in the glow of an epic orgasm.

"Val?" Meadow called out, the sound muffled by the bedroom door.

The unlocked door.

Val froze, and Asher groaned, "Think they'll go away?"

Which led to her giggling.

"Not funny," he grumbled but good-naturedly.

The situation held more embarrassment than humor, and yet she felt incredibly happy in that moment, if sticky. They both raced for the bathroom to indulge in a quick spot wash, her between the legs, and him, splashing his face.

As for his dick? Technically she'd sucked it clean. Her orgasm proved a little messier for him.

The man had a gift with his tongue. Pity they couldn't have indulged longer. She had a feeling he might be the man to finally give her multiples.

They hopped into clothes as fast as they could but not quick enough to avoid the knowing gazes when they emerged into the living room area of the penthouse.

Meadow grinned from ear to ear. Nova smirked. Poppy's cheeks bloomed. As for Rok, he nursed a beer that he set down the moment he saw Asher.

"Thank fuck you're here. Let's go hit the bar and casino."

Asher arched a brow. "Road trip that bad?"

"A man can only listen to so much giggling before he wants to shove an ice pick in his ear," was the grumble as Rok headed out the door, only to veer in an about-face. He stomped to Meadow, gave her a hard kiss, and muttered, "I'll see you in a few hours." He also squeezed her ass, which led to Meadow blushing bright but smiling.

Asher cast Val a glance, and she saw him debating if he should do the same.

"Don't you dare," she hissed, answering his question. They might have enjoyed really good oral sex, but she wasn't ready to act the part of couple, not in front of Meadow and company at any rate.

Once the boys left, the girls pounced.

"So, you and Asher?" Meadow ventured.

"Had a good time. Nothing else." A really good time that might need to be repeated. A few times.

"Sorry we interrupted," Nova snickered.

It was Poppy who saved Val from total embarrassment by saying, "Is anyone hungry? I brought brownies."

They spent the rest of that night eating brownies and cinnamon rolls and drinking the red wine Aunt Cecily brought up. She ended up staying and indulging with them.

Eventually, when the wine ran out, they all stumbled off to bed, including Val. She woke only briefly as Asher slid under the covers with her. She should probably tell him to take the couch lest people get the wrong idea.

Then again, they already had the wrong idea, and it was late. She snuggled into his spooning embrace and didn't wake until well past dawn. Alone.

Well, that sucked. She rose on her elbows and saw he'd left a note on the nightstand.

Just a phone call away if you need me, princess. See you later.

Not a declaration of love. Nor a pushy demand. Just a nice missive letting her know she wasn't forgotten. She tucked it into her purse, even as she inwardly berated herself for showing a weird senti-mentality.

The day proved hectic, but fun. Winnie came to the hotel with the baby and her mom and got along famously with everyone, even Aunt Cecily. After a morning of wedding shopping, they went for lunch in the restaurant while the baby napped alongside in a bassinet Cecily had brought in special for them.

That afternoon, while Winnie took the baby home for a good nap, there was yet more shopping, with Val acting as chauffeur in her SUV. They'd not seen the boys at all, although Val could have sworn she caught sight of Rok and even Asher a few times. Were they keeping tabs? Quite possibly. Maybe it was even prudent given the red-headed guy she'd seen twice now. One of Rocco's spies? She wouldn't put it past him. Val had no doubt that pencil dick would try something. His type couldn't stand being bested. Especially by a woman.

They met up with the boys for dinner, and Val could have gagged at the way her stomach clenched and her heart fluttered at the sight of Asher. Meadow had no compunction about throwing herself at Rok, who kissed her soundly. As for Asher, he didn't try anything so bold, but as they followed the group to dinner, he held her back rather than let her enter the restaurant. He pulled her behind a potted tree and murmured, "I've been dying to do this all day."

Before she could ask what, he kissed her. A long kiss that meant more knowing looks and grins as they rejoined the party. Let them smirk. The inner glow was well worth it.

Dinner proved a raucous affair that had Asher's family joining them. After dessert, Winnie and her mom left with the baby, but she insisted her husband remain with the boys to enjoy the impromptu bachelor party consisting of strippers and overpriced beer.

Not something Val found herself okay with, which led to Asher teasing before he left, "Don't worry, princess. None of them can hold a candle to you. I'll be tasting you later."

The promise didn't completely assuage her jealousy. Perhaps she should have hired some male strippers for their own event. *Bet he wouldn't be so blasé then.*

Rather than remain at their hotel, Aunt Cecily had arranged for them to be taken by limo to a rival's place. Giorgio—who also happened to be her part-time lover—greeted them. He was a handsome man in his late fifties with silver in his dark hair and a besotted look for Aunt Cecily. He started them off with enough tokens to cause some serious damage.

Meadow was positively giddy about getting to

play the slot machines. Laughing when she won. Giggling when she lost. At eight, they paused in order to enjoy the concert being put on by a local band and drank many tequila shots, then it was back to more gambling, for the other ladies at least. Val abstained because she'd noticed them being watched.

To lure out the spies, she hit the women's room and played Candy Crush on her phone. After fifteen minutes, Asher cautiously ventured in.

"Val? You okay?"

"No, I'm drowning in a toilet."

He ventured past the curved wall, apprehensive and with good reason. He shouldn't be in this women's-only space, especially since he sensed someone in one of the stalls.

Val sat at the vanity, meaning she saw him in the mirror and offered a lifted brow. "How did you end up here? I thought your plan involved cheap beer and strippers."

He shoved his hands into his pocket as he strolled closer and kept his voice low. "Turns out none of them are as hot as what we've already got. So rather than overpay for beer, we thought we'd play for some cash. Well, Rok and I did. Gordie went home to Winnie."

"And you just happened to end up at the same casino as us. Spying." She offered a sharp rebuttal rather than react to the part where he basically called her his.

"Think of it as a kill-two-birds-with-one stone scenario. We just wanted to make sure nothing bad happens."

"You're worried Rocco might pull a dumb stunt?"

A pause as he glanced at the closed door where a toilet flushed. "He's into some bad shit."

That brought a frown and she spun on the stool to face him directly. "Bad how?"

He clamped his mouth shut as the one occupied stall disgorged a woman, who shot Asher a dirty look as she passed. Only as the door shut did he quietly say, "Rumor has it that Rocco might be running illegal drugs."

"And where did you hear this rumor?"

He rolled his shoulders. "I might have done a bit of snooping today while you were out with the girls."

"Why?" It hit her the moment she asked. "Because of your family."

"I don't want anything happening to them, and with Rocco taking risks..." His lips turned down. "I have to do something."

"Such as? Are you going to gather evidence so you can take the matter to the police?"

A grimace tugged his lips. "I'd rather not get them involved."

A sentiment she could understand. "No one does, but keep in mind the cops won't go after your sister and her husband unless they're actively participating."

"I am aware. And they're not. However, the situation is a touch more complicated than that."

She said nothing, just waited.

He leaned against the vanity and sighed. "My family has secrets. Big ones. We don't need the police poking their nose in our affairs. Trust me when I saw it wouldn't be good."

"If you need a good lawyer, I can recommend a few."

"More family?"

"My uncle owes me a favor. I also know a problem solver, the kind that isn't afraid to take more drastic steps if you're really worried."

Some guys might have balked at her implication she condoned murder. Being a realist, Val knew sometimes there was only one way to truly solve a deplorable situation.

"The only thing that might help is if Rocco stepped in front of a bus."

"That could be arranged."

His eyes widened. "You're kidding, right?"

She smirked. "What do you think?" Always leave them wondering. Advice given by Aunt Margaret who had been married five times.

"Have I told you yet today how amazing you are, Valencia Berlusconi?"

"You're behind on your quota."

"Then let me rectify that." He pulled her to stand and tilted her chin. Before he could give her a kiss, someone entered and shot them a dirty look.

Val laughed. "I think that's our cue to leave. You going to join us gals since the jig is up?"

"Might as well. Maybe Rok will stop mooning if we do. The man has got it bad for your friend."

"I know." It was sweet and sickening all at once. She eyed him. "I swear, if you ever treat me like some porcelain doll—"

"You'll shoot me. Trust me, I know."

"Good. Now get out of here before someone calls security on the perv in the bathroom."

"Only a perv for you, princess," he said with a wink.

She laughed. "I don't know why I like you."

"It's because I am amazing."

"You're decent. Most of the time," she offered with a roll of her eyes.

"Killing me, princess."

"Oh, you'll die all right. Later, when we get back to the hotel." Words she purred against his mouth.

He shuddered. "Does it have to be later?"

"The party isn't over. Speaking of which, we should get back to them."

"Shall we?" He offered his arm, but she shook her head.

"I'll be a few minutes. I need to find out where my ejaculating penis cake went."

The expression on his face? Totally worth it.

"Um. Maybe Rok and I will join you after the cake."

Her grin proved wide as she clucked. "Chicken."

He leaned close to whisper, "More like tempted to show you the real thing."

There was only one reply for that. "Can't wait."

"Tease," he growled as he kissed her. Then he left, and she admired the view of his ass before freshening her lip gloss.

Time to track down that cake. She emerged from the washroom to run into a familiar, if unwanted, face.

"If it isn't Asher's supposed fiancée," Melinda said with a sneer.

"If it isn't the skank who cheated on her husband before their wedding," Val riposted.

"Virgin my ass. You've got slut written all over you."

Val offered a cold smile to the woman. "Takes one to know one."

The insult caused color to bloom in Melinda's face. "I'm married."

"And? I'm sure that hasn't stopped you."

"It won't stop Asher either. He's always had a thing for the ladies."

"Guess he hadn't met the right one to tame him." Val's barb hit the mark.

"He's using you," spat Melinda.

"Is he? Or am I using him?"

"He'll never marry you." A sharp retort that brought out the obstinate side of Val.

"He'd marry me tonight if I said yes. Now if you'll excuse me, I have a penis to track down." She held her chin high as she marched out, only to stumble as that bitch shoved her in the back.

Val hit the wall across from the women's wash-room before wheeling around. She glared at Melinda.

"Where's your protector now?" Melinda sassed.

"I don't need one. But you do." There was some-thing satisfying about hitting the other woman. Even better when she heard the crunch and yelp that said she'd broken a nose.

She could have added a few more slaps to the lesson of "Don't fuck with Val," but she had better things to do. That, however, didn't stop her from offering one last retort. "Good luck explaining to your husband why you felt a need to come after your ex-boyfriend's fiancée."

"Fucking cunt," Melinda managed to mumble as she held her bleeding nose.

The door to the bathroom opened, and whoever exited swung, knocking her unconscious.

SEVENTEEN

When Asher left Val, he sported a grin from ear to ear.

What a woman. He'd never been happier than when Winnie texted Gord saying she needed something called gripe water. With the man gone—and the strippers not catching their interest—Rok turned to him and said, "Wanna go check on the ladies?"

Fuck yeah, he did. Being away from Val gnawed at his innards and not because he feared for her safety. She should be fine given the size of her group in a secure casino. In case of a problem, Nova could kick ass, not to mention Val could handle herself.

Still, he itched to get back to her. He couldn't stop thinking about her. What they'd done. The pleasure...

Despite Asher having bathed, the scent of her clung to him. If he didn't know the claiming required fucking, he would have said it had already occurred because he felt a connection to her. A bond unlike anything he'd experienced before.

Which might explain his concern. Unease nagged him all day, especially once he realized what Rocco trafficked in. Gordie had proven helpful in that regard, concern for his new family leading him to tell Asher about the things he'd seen as Pack accountant. Inconsistencies in the receipts. A lack of explanation for some of the invoices. The drugs he'd smelled when he'd gone by a warehouse Rocco managed to retrieve some paperwork.

It appeared Kit was right. Something putrid was apaw in the Festivus Pack. He'd texted his findings thus far to Kit. The man didn't reply, but no doubt he'd relay Asher's report.

What would the Lykosium do? If Rocco were involved in the illegal drug trade, Asher could see them coming down hard and making an example. But how deep did the rot go? Was Bruce involved? Some or most of the Pack?

Not his problem. He'd done as asked, and he should have been relieved to know Rocco would be handled. It would lessen the threat he posed.

The dead-end hallway that held the washrooms led to the casino proper, where he made his way to a poker table. Asher almost chuckled at the sight of Nova scowling by her small pile of chips, while Poppy clapped her hands, probably because her stack just got bigger.

"I won again!"

"How is that possible?" Nova complained. "You learned how to play like five minutes ago."

"Guess I'm just lucky."

No, Asher was the lucky one for finding the one woman who made him feel complete.

Nova spotted him and snorted. "Aha, there's co-dependent number two."

"What's that supposed to mean?"

Nova jerked her head toward Rok, who stood by Meadow's chair, where she pulled a lever and then bounced in excitement as the spinning wheels slowed to a stop. Rok's sappy expression brought a grimace to Asher's face.

"I am not that bad," he grumbled.

"Yet, but it's coming. You are so head over heels for her it's gross."

His lips twisted. "Is it that obvious?"

"Just a little."

Nova might have teased more if Aunt Cecily

hadn't clapped her hands and bellowed louder than the clanging bells, "Bachelorette party, it's cake time. Get the bride-to-be over here."

As Asher and the others neared the massive table—able to seat a comfortable twelve if you didn't mind sliding along the round leather banquette—reserved for their party, he noticed Val had yet to join them. What kept her? Because it sure as fuck wasn't the cake, which arrived in its erect splendor, sending Meadow into a giggling fit, Nova grimacing, Rok looking everywhere but at the cake, and Poppy beet red.

As for Asher, that nagging foreboding turned into full-blown panic.

Danger.

He veered from the party and almost ran back to the washrooms, panicking for nothing. It had only been a few minutes since he'd left her.

Long enough for Val to disappear, leaving only her scent behind, hers and that of a Were female. One he recognized.

Melinda. The familiar aroma clenched his stomach. What did she want with Val? Didn't matter. If she'd harmed a single fucking hair...

His lip pulled back in a snarl as he strode down the hall to the exit doors. A sign warned, *Exit under surveillance. An alarm will sound if opened.*

A glance overhead showed the camera pointing in the wrong direction. Slamming open the door, not a single noise gave warning. Someone had disabled the security.

His gut tightened further.

He exited to find himself in an asphalt parking lot. No Val. No Melinda. Nothing but receding tail-lights and a door that locked behind him.

Fuck. He stood for a moment, hands on his hips, glancing left and right. Could be he panicked for nothing. Maybe Val and Melinda simply had a chat and got stuck outside. Maybe Val had to take the long way around to get back in.

He knew that was wishful thinking, given he couldn't locate her scent. Idiot. He should try calling. He pulled out his phone and dialed her number.

It rang four times and went to voicemail. Didn't mean something bad had happened. His wolf sense claimed otherwise.

He called again, and this time it was answered by the wrong person.

"That didn't take you long."

Hearing Rocco's voice sent a chill through Asher. "What have you done with Val?"

"Nothing yet. But don't worry, by the time she returns to you, she'll be well used. Just like my fucking wife was."

"Don't you fucking dare drag Val into this. Especially since you know Melinda was willing."

"Yours will be too once I soften her up with a special blend of drugs."

"Don't you dare."

"Too late. I've got her, and there's nothing you can do about it."

"You're a fucking bastard."

"Fucking yes. And maybe you'll get lucky and have to raise my bastard." Rocco hung up, and Asher threw his phone in a rare fit of rage before angrily pacing.

Now what? Save Val, of course. Where would Rocco have taken her?

He bent over, his hands flat on his thighs, and took a few deep breaths.

Think.

He couldn't think. Panic filled him. Rocco had Val. And the longer he had her, the less likely Asher would be able to rescue her unharmed.

The exit door had slammed shut behind him, and rather than go around, he retrieved his now cracked phone and called Rok.

The moment his Alpha answered, he spilled the problem in a rush. "Pack leader's son took Val as payback for shit that went down a long time ago. I have to get her back."

"Where are you?"

It was tempting to tell Rok and have him by his side; however, involving the Alpha of a rival Pack would start a war. Not that Rok would care, which was the problem. He redirected Rok's attention. "I don't know if they're targeting anyone else close to me. You should get the ladies to safety."

"Nova can take care of them."

"Once they're back in the penthouse, yes, but given I was ambushed on the way there yesterday with Val, you shouldn't take any chances."

Rok didn't refute but did ask, "Where has he taken her?"

"I don't know." Asher realized there was probably only one place Rocco would use for this kind of nefarious deed. "I gotta go. I'll text you when I figure out the location."

"Asher, don't go alone."

"Not planning to. About to contact my backup now." His backup being Kit. But first, he had to get a hold of Gordie.

When his brother-in-law answered, he said, "I need the address of the warehouse Rocco's using."

Gordie hesitated before giving him the information and adding, "Why?"

No point in lying. "Rocco took Val." Then he hung up and texted Kit and Rok.

Kit didn't reply, but Rok had a brief message: *Wait for me.*

Asher couldn't. Not with Val in danger.

I'm coming, princess.

EIGHTEEN

Waking up in the trunk of a car? Not how Val planned to have her evening end, but she didn't panic despite the temptation. This wasn't the first time she'd gotten trapped in this fashion.

Aunt Kiki used to own a salvage yard and made it a point to teach a young Val how to escape if she was ever trapped against her will. Aunt Kiki watched a lot of true crime shows.

Most cars built after 2002 possessed a release mechanism inside the trunk. If she could just find it...

Val groped in the dark to locate the button. Once found, it was simply a matter of waiting for the vehicle to slow or stop for a light.

While she waited, she cursed herself for being stupid. It never occurred to her that Melinda might have a friend in cahoots with her. Had the abduction been planned or spur of the moment?

Didn't matter given the end result.

A kidnapped Val stuck listening to shitty music blaring from the car speakers. It boom-boomed in time to the throbbing of her head. In good news, it would hide any noise she made when she escaped.

The car slowed to a stop.

Click. The lid popped open, and Val spilled out of the car, hitting the pavement hard. Fuck the pain, though. Number one rule of survival: Get away at all costs.

She got to her feet and ran. She was still in the city, if a more industrial part of it. Not exactly great, as it meant little traffic. In good news, there were plenty of shadowy spots to hide. She bolted for the nearest building, wanting to get out of sight. She rounded the corner and leaned against the concrete, doing her best to control her breathing. Despite the loud music, her abductors had already noticed her escape. Stupid warning light on the dash probably gave it away.

Car doors slammed, and she heard voices.

"You said she was out cold." Rocco's voice.

"Bitch must have woken up." Melinda's sulky reply.

A husband and wife who abducted together.

How cute. Terrifying. Fuck. She patted her pockets looking for her phone.

Gone.

No weapon either. A rare occasion. Stupid fucking casinos and their bloody metal detectors. She'd left her gun at the hotel, never imagining a night out with a group of women would be dangerous.

Her best hope? Hide until they got tired of looking and left. Then she'd find a way to contact Meadow. Or Asher. He'd be so pissed.

Hell, she was pissed. How dare those fuckers drag her into their stupid vendetta. If Rocco wanted to be mad, then he should try blaming his wife.

She didn't hear them talking. Heard nothing at all as a matter of fact. Not even the purr of the car engine. She counted to a hundred and then peeked around the corner.

The car was gone.

She heaved out a breath of relief but didn't leave her hiding spot. They might have parked out of sight, hoping she'd reveal herself.

Leaning against the wall, she closed her eyes, not thinking of her aching head or the fact she'd been kidnapped, because both of those things sucked. She focused instead on the man who made her feel things she'd never expected. Made her want a life she'd previously eschewed.

Val had fully expected to turn into her Aunt Cecily, a single businesswoman for life. Now...she wasn't so sure.

A scuff from the back of the building made her turn. At first, she saw nothing, and then a pair of eyes reflected, white and glowing. The shadowy shape neared. Bigger than a rat. Taller than a cat.

She held her breath as if it would make her invisible to the creature stalking closer. It padded quietly and got close enough she managed to make out its shape in the gloom. A giant dog. Probably feral if it was out alone in this place at night.

It growled.

She backed away, not daring to take her eyes off of it. It crept closer, and she stepped from the concealment of the building onto the concrete sidewalk lining the road.

It followed, and she realized she looked upon a wolf, not a dog. A big fucker, too, with brown fur streaked with lighter strands and massive teeth that glistened when it snarled.

The distraction meant she never noticed the man at her back, who wrapped an arm around her neck and whispered, "Gotcha!"

She fought. Slammed her head back and heard a

satisfying crunch. She rammed her foot down even as her elbow jabbed into his gut. Rocco loosened his grip, and she tore free, only to wobble as she faced a naked woman. The shock of it had her gaping, long enough that she couldn't avoid the second blow to her head.

The next time Val woke, her head pounded but her wrists hurt the most. Probably on account she was tied to a chair set in the middle of a cavernous space.

In the dim illumination, she noticed stacked crates and a forklift currently not in use. A warehouse then. Not good. Only one reason to have her bound in such a place.

"At last, she wakes. About time. I've been waiting. It's not fun if you're not awake to scream." Rocco strutted from between some wooden boxes, shirtless, the top button on his pants undone. Oh fuck.

She pulled at the ties binding her. "Let me go."

"So soon? But the fun hasn't even started." He stopped in front of her, an evil tilt to his lips.

"I don't know what sick game you're playing, but it needs to stop right now. Whatever your problem is with Asher, take it up with him." She tried to sound braver than she felt.

Rocco crouched. "This is me handling my issue with that pretty-boy fucker. He defiled something of mine. I just plan to repay the favor. That's it. Once we're done here, you can go running back to your lover. Although, once he smells what I've done, I doubt you'll be together for long."

Fear iced her veins. The helpless kind she hated. "There is something seriously wrong with you."

"Actually, I'm very well formed. All the women say so." He stood and puffed out his chest.

"Is that why your wife had to go looking elsewhere?" Not the brightest thing to say, but she wasn't about to cower before this fucker.

His mouth flattened. "Melinda regrets that choice, and as part of her ongoing apology, she was the one to suggest an equitable outcome."

"Raping me isn't equitable," she almost yelled, rocking in the seat, frustrated when nothing loosened or budged.

"I want Asher to feel what I did. To know that he's not the first to put his cock inside you."

"Think again, fucker. You'll be lucky if you even have a cock once I'm done with you." The threat emerged in a low growl as Asher stepped from between some crates.

Her eyes widened, but not as much as Rocco's, although he hid his surprise when he whirled to face Asher. "How did you find me?"

"Did you really think I wouldn't be able to track my mate?" Asher snarled.

"She's not your mate, yet," Rocco refuted.

"She is in every way that counts, and even if she weren't, what you're about to do is a crime punishable by death."

Wait, what? She'd not taken Asher for the violent type, and yet he appeared so very dangerous as he stalked closer. He bristled head to toe. His eyes flashed, and for a moment, he had a primal nature about him that gave her a shiver.

"Only punishable if someone finds out," Rocco taunted.

"Is a video evidence enough?" Asher held up his phone. "I hit Send, and they will know."

They who? He must be talking about the cops.

"I can't let you do that." A new voice entered the fray. A man she'd seen at the baby christening appeared.

Asher whirled. "Don't interfere, Bruce. I only called you here to witness your son's depravity in person since you apparently haven't been paying attention."

"I knew," Bruce softly admitted.

"And did nothing to curb him?" Asher sounded genuinely disappointed.

"Life's been hard since the oil boom days fled. A

leader's gotta do what he must to keep his people afloat."

"By running drugs?"

"Never said I agreed. However, as next in line, Rocco's got a right to choose the direction the Pack will go in."

"A direction that includes kidnapping and rape?"

Bruce's jaw tightened. "You know I would never condone that."

"Do I? Because the Alpha I knew growing up was an honest man. He would have never been the type to deal in illegal drugs or to let anyone, even his son, hurt a woman."

"Just your woman. And you know why."

"You can't seriously be blaming me for the actions of your fucked-up son."

"Nothing would have happened if you'd just stayed away. Why did you have to return?" Bruce shook his head.

"Trust me, I'm wishing I hadn't. The Alpha I used to know was a good man. The kind who would never condone this." Asher chided, and Bruce physically shrank in shame.

"I never expected things to end up like this," a weary admission from Bruce.

"Are you fucking kidding me?" Rocco snapped. "You weren't whining at the extra cash I brought in."

"I was weak and wrong." Bruce hung his head before turning a burning glare on his son. "I should have put a stop to your antics a long time ago. But I didn't, and I'll have to live with that. But enough is enough. This time you've gone too far."

At the rebuke, Rocco sneered. "Don't like it? Too bad. You know where the door is."

"You might want to listen to your Alpha, given how bad things are already looking for you." Yet another stranger emerged, but this one brought relief to Asher's face.

"Kit, thank fuck. I was wondering if you got my messages."

"Who are you?" Rocco bristled, puffing up in a way that was alarming.

Even Bruce's eyes took on a hard glint. "You're trespassing in things that don't concern you, stranger."

"On the contrary. Your actions *are* my concern. I'm here on official business. In case there's any doubt..." Kit flashed something that deflated Bruce.

"Fuck me. The council sent you." The older man slumped.

But Rocco wasn't caving to whoever this Kit person was. Criminals seldom gave up quietly. "I don't give a flying fuck who this prick works for. We own this territory."

"Only by the grace of the Lykosium," Bruce said, confusing Val. What was the Lykosium?

"Fuck the council!" Rocco declared.

"Watch your mouth around the enforcer, you fucking lackwit." His dad finally showed signs of losing his temper.

"Or what? What's one asshole think he can do?" Rocco focused on Kit. "Maybe you need a lesson on why you shouldn't stick your nose in other people's business." Rocco cracked his knuckles, and it wasn't just Asher's brows that rose.

Kit sounded incredulous. "Are you that stupid you'd threaten me?"

"He didn't mean it." Bruce hastened to defuse the situation.

Only Rocco wouldn't have it. "Hell yeah, I am threatening. No, make that a promise. You will regret sticking your nose in my affairs."

Kit's coat gaped enough that she saw the holster within. He had a gun. "It would seem my presence here was warranted. You've broken quite a few laws, Rocco Durante."

Definitely sounded like a cop, only why was he confronting Rocco alone? Something about the situation didn't ring true, and she frowned. Blame her throbbing head for missing the clue that would make sense of it all.

"Way I see it, no one will know shit if you're not able to report." Rocco doubled down.

"You think you can kill me?" Kit sneered. "You and what army?"

"Way I see it, it's three against one."

Asher shook his head. "Like fuck am I siding with you. Who do you think called Kit?"

"Traitor!" Rocco spat. "Let's see if you change your mind once your precious enforcer has no choice but to kill your human whore. Because you know the laws state we can't have an unbound human running around who knows our secret."

What secret? Was this still about the drugs or...

Why was Rocco shoving down his pants?

Her eyes widened as suddenly Rocco's flesh rippled. His bare torso sprouted fur, his limbs shifted, losing their shape and becoming something else. The transformation took seconds.

She blinked.

But the fact remained. Rocco had become a massive wolf.

NINETEEN

A SHITTY SITUATION DEVOLVED INTO A veritable nightmare as Rocco purposely exposed the Were secret in front of the very human Val, exploiting the flaw in their laws that eliminated humans who knew. Someone really should do something about unscrupulous types like Rocco, who abused it to rid themselves of people.

Kit's mouth tightened. "I really wish he'd not done that." He reached inside his coat, and Asher's belly tightened as a gun emerged.

Who was Kit planning to shoot?

Just in case it was Val, the only non-Were, Asher stood in front of the man. "Let's not act rash now."

"A little too late for that," Kit snapped. "Move. Or do you want to see your woman getting eaten?"

What? Asher whirled in time to see a growling Rocco advancing on Val.

Bruce proved to be useless, yelling, "Rocco, no!" As if the fucker would start listening to his dad now.

"I've had quite enough of this circus," Kit muttered, aiming his weapon.

Only, when he would have fired, Bruce tackled him, sending the shot awry. The discharge of the gun distracted Rocco, but only for a second. Long enough for Asher to run for him while unbuttoning his pants and kicking off his shoes.

He'd just shed his shirt as Rocco resumed stalking toward Val, who was still bound and in clear shock.

"Why not fight someone your own kind?" Asher yelled.

Rocco paused long enough to eye him over a furry shoulder. He huffed hotly in mockery. Fucking bastard just wouldn't accept he'd lost. Not without causing more harm first.

Rocco leaped for Val!

Asher had run out of time. He still wore pants but didn't care. He exploded, his remaining clothes shredding with the urgency of his shift because he knew his fleshy human form didn't stand a chance against a full-grown wolf in a fight. He had to save Val, yet he proved a second too late. Rocco slammed into her and tilted the chair. She hit the floor on her back and uttered a short grunt.

A gunshot cracked, and Rocco turned his head slightly, the pause enough for Asher to take a bounding leap. He plowed into Rocco before the other wolf could tear out Val's throat. The momentum sent them both tumbling.

Forget the movies with their musical scores and slow-motion imagery. A wolf fight lacked grace. Technique didn't exactly come into play. Their very shapes locked them into a tough battle that involved paws tipped in claws and elongated muzzles with teeth meant for tearing. It came down to being a test of strength and endurance that involved much snarling and snapping. Grappling to see who could get a better hold.

A neck grip would end the fight. A fight Asher couldn't lose.

He could hear Val's panting as she struggled to get free. The chair hadn't broken, but the rope around her upper body had shifted and loosened.

With a sudden jerk, Rocco rolled away from Asher and scrabbled on the concrete floor in Val's direction. The bastard lunged, mouth open to latch onto her.

Val yelled, "Like fuck!" She kicked Rocco's

muzzle when he would have clamped on. Then slammed her foot again, shoving him back.

It allowed Asher to get close enough to bite down on a hind leg and drag the fucker away from Val. He growled and shook his head as he pulled, taking rare glee in Rocco's yip of pain.

Rocco twisted, and Asher lost his grip, though he still tore Rocco's flesh as he turned away. Wounded. Asher pressed him harder, landing more bites, dominating the wrestling. The pair of them huffed with exertion before Asher straddled Rocco and put his teeth on the other wolf's neck.

He could end it now if he wanted. Stop this horrible excuse for a person from ever harming anyone else.

Bruce yelled, "Don't kill my son." The plea of a father who loved his only child. A man who'd ignored the crimes Rocco committed.

Killing Rocco would do the world a favor. Bruce, too. He could then stop covering for his son.

The pressure in Asher's jaw increased, crushing the neck in his grip. Rocco panicked and thrashed, but Asher held him too firmly. He would have killed him, but he caught sight of Val staring at him. She'd managed to get out of the chair and sat, her head turned, ignoring Kit, who sawed through the rope holding her wrists bound.

He didn't want her to see any more violence. Bad enough she probably already thought he was a monster. Better to let Kit arrest Rocco's ass and drag him back to the Lykosium for trial and execution. Some crimes were too grave to forgive.

Asher pushed away from the heaving body on the floor. Wondered how much blood matted his fur. Val had yet to say anything, but she stood, accepting Kit's offered grip, stumbling slightly into him before recovering.

Kit returned his knife to the strap on his empty holster. He must have lost his gun.

Still in his wolf shape, Asher took a step in Val's direction. She didn't flinch, but her lips did flatten. Her gaze narrowed.

Definitely not happy with him, but at least she showed no fear.

Suddenly, her eyes widened, and her mouth parted. "Asher, behind you!"

It appeared Rocco hadn't given up. Asher whirled and prepared to meet the challenge. He heard the gunshot before he saw the effect.

A hole appeared between Rocco's eyes. Kill shot. The wolf dropped to the ground, dead.

"My son," Bruce sobbed, running for the body.

Hard to feel bad for him given he was partially to

blame for Rocco's demise. If only Bruce had reined Rocco in earlier before he'd gotten so depraved.

As to who fired that shot?

Kit frowned at Val. "You stole my gun."

She appeared unapologetic. "I evened the odds."

"Give it back." Kit held out his hand, only to receive an icy glare.

"I don't think so." Not the best reply given who Kit represented.

"Keep it then. I'll deal with you later." Kit moved in Bruce's direction. The man knelt by Rocco's body, sobbing openly.

Asher shifted back to his two-legged shape. Why not? It wasn't as if he could hide what he was. Not anymore. He at least wanted to be able to explain. "Val, I—"

"Would you put something on? I am not talking to you about anything while your dick is dangling." She looked away from him.

He halted in shock. "Um. Sorry." A glance around showed the closest thing was his ruined pants. Weres often forgot how prudish humans could get about nudity. He tied the scraps over his junk. "Is this better?"

"Barely."

"If you're feeling overdressed, you could take

your clothes off." At the expression on her face, he offered a sheepish, "Too soon?"

"Way too soon to be acting blasé. What the fuck is going on, Asher?"

"It's complicated."

"Complicated is you being married to someone else. This is fucking insane."

"It's—"

The interruption came in the form of a screech. "You killed my husband!" Melinda emerged from between the stacks, swinging a metal bar that never connected.

Bang.

Melinda hit the ground, screaming in pain from the hole in her leg and then cursing out the person who shot her. "You cunt! How dare you try and kill me."

"If I wanted you dead, you'd have a hole in your head to match your husband." Val had never appeared fiercer.

"Fucking human. I am going to gut you," Melinda hissed.

Showing entirely too much calm, Val walked over and put the muzzle to Melinda's forehead. "You are really tempting me to shut that shrill mouth permanently."

Wisely, Melinda zipped her trap. She clutched her leg and glared.

Val perused the area and, as if satisfied the threats had been handled, tucked the gun in her waistband before she headed for him.

He smiled. "Princess, I'm—"

He should have expected the slap.

TWENTY

Anger coursed through Val. That lying fucker. Talk about a furry whopper of a secret.

Fear iced her veins, too. Because she'd almost died.

Mixed in there was amazement because, holy shit, werewolves existed. Including Asher, who went from wolf to naked man, grabbing the scraps of his pants to tie around his waist to hide his junk. That still left most of him bare. He must be cold without his fur.

Fucking fur.

She still couldn't believe it. When Rocco had changed into a wolf, she first thought they'd drugged her. Only it turned out to be real.

Too real. Then Asher changed, and what tether she had on her sanity and emotions snapped.

She slapped Asher.

It felt good, so she punched him in the gut next. Like hitting a bloody wall.

She went nose to nose with him and snapped, "What the fuck? How could you not tell me you're some raging beast?"

"If I was raging, it was only because you were in danger." A soft reply that deflated her ire.

"I can defend myself."

"So I saw."

Since she couldn't gauge how he actually felt about her killing someone, she added a huffy, "It was self-defense."

"I know. I was there, remember?"

"I wouldn't have had to do anything if you'd taken care of him," she complained. Initially, it appeared as if Asher would kill Rocco. Then, just when he literally had the other wolf by the throat, he walked away.

"I worried you'd freak out if you saw me kill a man."

"That wasn't a man." Flatly said. His lips pinched, and she added, "Psychos, no matter their shape, can't be allowed to roam free."

"I'll remember that for next time." He glanced at Melinda, who was bitching as Kit tied her hands rather than tending to her wound. "Surprised you let her live."

"In order to avoid charges, someone close to Rocco might be needed to confess all his sins."

"We can't go to the cops."

"Guess not." Because how exactly could they explain a dead wolf who appeared to be turning slowly back into a human? Freaky. She shivered.

"You okay?"

"Not really." The admission slipped from her before she could stop it.

When he would have taken her in his arms, she moved out of reach, not ready yet. She had questions. "How come you never told me about your animal thing?"

"Exactly how would that conversation have gone? Dear princess, I'm a werewolf who likes his steak medium, not rare, and loves to run four-legged and furry under a full moon."

"This isn't funny."

"Agreed."

She glanced at his stony expression. Not a hint of humor to be seen. "This is seriously messed up."

"It is."

She wanted to yell, but his soft replies made it impossible. Worse, she couldn't stay mad at him. She scrubbed a hand over her face. "I need some wine. A vat of it. And some serious sugary treats because you've got lots of explaining to do."

"I promise. I'll tell you everything once I get you back to the hotel."

Which was when Bruce, possibly a worse father than her own, felt a need to waste air. "Hold on a second. The human can't leave. She's not oathbound." Bruce pointed accusingly at her.

Given a lot of the blame for Rocco's actions lay at his feet, she had to resist a temptation to pull the gun and show him what she thought of his parenting skills.

Before she could impress with her aim, Asher blasted to her defense. "No shit she's not oathbound because she wasn't supposed to find out like this. You can blame your son for that."

"Doesn't change the fact she knows and is a liability. She has to be dealt with now." Bruce doubled down on his stubborn asshattery.

Bristling with anger, Asher snapped right back. "I'll deal with my mate."

Bruce sneered. "Doesn't matter what she is. Humans must be oathbound to know our secret, or else face the consequences. The law is the law, right, enforcer?" He turned to Kit, who appeared to be texting.

"You are really a piece of work," Kit muttered in reply. "I see where the son got it from."

"But I'm right." Bruce appeared triumphant.

Asher turned pale.

"What's he talking about? What's this oath thing? Why is it a big deal?" Because she remained lost in this conversation.

Asher's jaw shifted, and his word bit out tight. "It's a binding promise a human makes to keep them from being able to tell others about us."

"Us as in werewolves, in the plural? Because you and Rocco are obviously not the only ones."

He nodded.

Werewolves existed. How many exactly? Didn't matter. She didn't have a choice.

She blew out a hard breath. "You want me to swear I won't tell? Fine. Your secret is safe with me. As if anyone would believe me anyhow." The last was muttered under her breath.

"It's not that simple," Asher stated. "You need to give your vow to an Alpha for the magic to work."

"Magic?" She snorted. Then again, her disbelief might be misplaced given what she'd just seen.

"Good luck finding one in time because I ain't helping you." Bruce continued to be an epic dick.

Kit ignored them all to stalk down the crawling

Melinda, who didn't let her bound wrists and ankles stop her.

"Am I too late?" Rok stepped into view.

Meadow appeared shaken but clung to his side. Nova and Poppy flanked them, the latter being the most surprising with her fierce expression.

"This doesn't involve you, Fleetfoot." Bruce focused his ire on the new arrivals.

"I disagree. He"—Amarok inclined his head in Asher's direction—"belongs to me."

"But he broke the rules in my territory," Bruce snarled.

"Not yours, actually," Kit declared, rising from Melinda's turkey-bound body, her wrists now attached to her ankles. "As emissary to the Lykosium, and enforcer of their laws, I declare the Festivus Pack to be under Lykosium conservatorship until such a time as you have answered for your crimes and those of your departed son."

"You can't do that. I knew nothing of Rocco's plans," Bruce blustered.

"Meaning you either willfully ignored what happened under your nose or were too dumb to see it happening. Which is it?" Kit's dryly replied.

"I won't be imprisoned," Bruce declared.

"That's not up to you."

When Bruce would have bolted, Nova tackled him and took the tie wraps Kit handed over to truss him. No one appeared all that shocked at the events unfolding more dramatically than any soap opera.

As Val eyed them all, she suddenly realized something. "Holy fuck, you're all in cahoots." She glanced at Meadow biting her lower lip. "Even you. You knew about this wolf thing."

"I'm sorry. I couldn't tell you."

"I'm your best friend." It burst out angry to hide the hurt.

Which was when Rok stepped in front of Meadow as if to shield her. "Don't blame her. She made a promise to me and kept it."

"And exactly who is the real you? Because you're obviously not just some ranch owner."

"I am Alpha to the Feral Pack."

"Feral?" Val arched a brow. "Meaning what? You're rabid killers?"

"Couldn't be further from the truth. And I can explain." Rok cleared his throat and looked away for a second. A bit of ruddy color stained his face. "I was drunk when our Pack name was chosen."

"But it's perfect because every single one of the people in our Pack would go feral on anyone who dared hurt one of us," Nova drawled.

"They're good people," Meadow stated, her chin angled high.

Val homed in on Meadow. "Jeezus, you're one of them, too. I was right. You are in a cult!"

Everyone stared at Val with shocked expressions. Nova broke the silence with a guffaw. "Guess we are."

"We're thinking of making our Pack slogan, 'Join us because we serve the best cookies,'" Poppy added.

"This is nuts," Val muttered.

"Would it help if I said we don't lick them?" Asher tried to lighten the mood.

She glared. "Still too early for jokes." She refused to even think of the fact he'd alluded to them licking their balls. Ew. Instead, she focused on something else. "Amarok told Bruce you belonged to him. What's that mean?"

Rok replied, "Asher is my Beta. My right-hand guy." Making him important in the hierarchy by the sounds of it.

"We all have our roles," Asher added.

"I'm the resident lesbian bitch," Nova said with a wink.

"This is too much weird for one day." Val went to leave, only for Kit to block the exit. She had no patience left. "Out of my way."

"I'm afraid our business isn't quite concluded."

"Maybe yours isn't, but I'm done." She pulled the gun she'd kept. "Move."

It was Asher's soft words that stopped her. "You can't leave quite yet, princess."

"Can't?" She whirled and aimed the weapon at Asher. "You going to stop me?"

"If I have to. I'd rather you not make me."

"Make you? So much for feeling something for me," she said on a sneer.

"Even for you, there are some rules I can't break." Asher looked stricken. His shoulders rounded in a slump.

"You should listen to your mate, Valencia Berlusconi." Kit was the one to speak.

"Or what?" she snapped at the redhead.

"While I do recognize the situation is not of your doing, understand I will kill you to protect the Were secret."

She eyed Kit. Saw her death in his gaze. He'd do it. Without a qualm.

She turned to Amarok. "Someone said I needed to swear to an Alpha. Will you do?"

He nodded.

"Any special speech required?"

"Just state your oath aloud."

Through stiff lips, Val uttered her vow. "I promise I won't ever tell anyone about the facts smelly werewolves exist, or that my best friend is marrying a flea-ridden beast, or that my dumb ass slept with a hairy, lying dog. Happy?" She finished with a glare.

"I accept your oath," Rok said in a low, somber tone.

A zing went through her. She frowned, but everyone else appeared relieved. "So is that it? I promised so now I'm free to go?"

Kit stepped aside in reply.

She stalked out of the warehouse and heard someone following. It wasn't Asher at her heels but Meadow.

"Val, slow down. Now that you're oathbound, I can explain."

"Now you can?" She whipped around. "What about before when I was worried you were marrying into some cult? Only to find out it *is* a cult, and a weird one."

"They're really good people."

"I'm sure they are. With the mother of all secrets. For fuck's sake, Meadow. You weren't there to see it. They're beasts. When Asher and Rocco fought..." She paused, remembering the savagery in that moment. She raked fingers through her hair. "Jeezus, I need some wine."

"We all could use a glass I think." Nova emerged and dangled Val's keys. "You might need these to get anywhere, though."

"The boys said we should go back to the hotel while they clean up." A pale Poppy emerged, hugging herself.

Val held out her hand. "What are we waiting for?"

Nova tucked the keys close. "I'm driving."

"My car," Val argued.

"You're in no state to be behind the wheel."

Given the throb in her head, Val couldn't entirely disagree. At least Nova knew how to properly speed and went faster when Poppy exclaimed, "Slow down." Meadow sat in the back with Val, holding her hand, not saying anything yet. Good, because Val was still processing all that had happened.

In no time they were in the penthouse and ordering up booze and food.

Val sank onto the couch and sighed. "What a night."

"Are you okay?" Meadow asked tentatively, which was unlike her usual bubbly nature.

She cracked an eye to glare. "I still can't believe

you kept the werewolf thing from me."

"I had no choice."

"Because they swore you to secrecy. So much for the best-friend oath." Val grimaced. "Speaking of secrets, what happened to my aunt?" Last she'd seen her was at the casino.

"We told her you and Asher had gone off to be young and romantic, and when we claimed it was bedtime, she opted to stay with her boyfriend at the casino."

"Good." It meant her aunt had no idea of the mess she'd somehow fallen into.

"Want to talk about what happened?" Poppy tendered a soft invitation.

"Not yet." Although she did have one pressing question. "How was the cake?"

The video they played had her laughing. Especially given the look of horror on Rok's face as some of the whipped cream filling that shot out of the dick treat hit him, too.

Val didn't stay up long after that, dragging herself to bed and telling Meadow to fuck off with her whole "I'm gonna wake you every two hours." She didn't have a concussion. What she had was a sore heart, because the one guy she thought she had feelings for turned out to be someone else.

A man with a hairy secret, who'd come to her defense.

Which might be why when she woke in the morning and saw him sleeping at the foot of her bed, rather than shoot him with the gun under her pillow, she drawled, "No doggies on the bed."

TWENTY-ONE

NOT EXACTLY THE BEST OF GREETINGS, BUT Asher took it as a positive sign that maybe he could settle things with Val.

When Val left the previous evening, all he wanted to do was follow; however, duty called. A duty that started with disposing of the body caught mid-shift. If left alone, it might eventually become fully human. Not a chance they could take. It became part of the burning inferno that also destroyed all the drugs. But they didn't set the warehouse aflame until they'd transferred all the computer hard drives and files to Kit's dark sedan parked a few blocks away.

At least they'd didn't have to worry about any cameras cataloguing their moves. Rocco showed some rare sense in his business placement. Once the warehouse burned, with no hope of the firefighters finding anything but ash and bone fragments, Asher and Amarok accompanied Kit to the airport, using Rocco's car. Once Kit left, it would be taken to a junkyard for crushing.

As they helped load the private jet with bodies and evidence of Rocco's crimes, Kit took Asher aside. "The Festivus Pack needs someone to guide them while a new Alpha is chosen."

"Not me." He said it even as he heard the request in Kit's voice.

"Yes you. At least until we can find someone suitable."

"Ask Rok. He's good at bossing people around."

"He has his own Pack to manage."

"Exactly. A Pack where I'm his Beta."

"One of two. This kind of inter-Pack aid is exactly the kind of thing expected of someone in your position."

"I can't just up and move. Rok's getting married in like a week."

"No one said you couldn't visit. Or that you couldn't delegate. That fellow Gordie seems like he's decent. And I'm sure your sister would enjoy having you around for a while."

He grimaced. "Way to guilt me."

"It's not guilt. It's called you having a moral

conscience. It seems to be in rare supply for some Packs these days." Kit signaled the pilots, who shut the cargo area and got onto the plane to get it ready for departure.

"Being the boss is a lot of work. I don't know if I want that kind of responsibility permanently."

"It would be for a few weeks, months at most. Just settle any squabbles and make sure no one does anything stupid."

"And what of Val?"

"What about her? Your mate. Your problem."

When did his life get so complicated?

The reason glared at him, looking rumpled and beautiful. And annoyed.

It made his decision when he arrived at the penthouse late a good one. Rather than disturb her by crawling into bed beside her, he'd tucked into the ample room at the foot.

He stretched and drawled, "I promise I won't shed."

"I don't sleep with animals."

"Does it help if I say my shots are up to date?"

"I hate dogs."

"Good thing I'm a wolf then."

She pursed her lips. "This isn't funny."

"No, it's not, which is why we should probably talk about it."

"You mean discuss the fact you've been lying to me."

"Not by choice. Surely you can see why we keep it a secret."

"I'm not stupid. Obviously, you can't tell just anyone." Left unsaid in her sulky tone was, why didn't he think her worthy?

"I've been wanting to tell you, but we met only a few days ago, and there hasn't really been the right time. Then last night happened—"

"Do you often engage in battles to the death?"

"No. Last night is not the norm for our kind."

"You mean you're not all a bunch of megalomaniacs who like to kidnap and torture women?"

His lips quirked. "We are arrogant, but psychos like Rocco are rare."

"Not really given I met his wife. Cuckoo." She spun a finger by the side of her head. "Gotta say, I think you dodged a bullet there."

He shuddered. "No shit." He paused before saying, "So how much did you learn last night?"

"Not much because, quite honestly, I just wanted to get pleasantly buzzed and go to bed. Although discussing the whole werewolf thing has reminded me I should invest in silver in case word ever gets out."

"I already did." He grinned. "It was Reece's

suggestion when a video emerged last year. We thought our secret was done for, but the Lykosium Council managed to get it discredited."

"They are..." she prodded.

"The ones keeping the Packs, and their members, in line."

"Indicating a level of government. Fuck." She leaned back against the pillows. "I can't believe you howl at the moon." She bit her lower lip. "Is it contagious?"

"Nope. We're born this way."

"Born?" Her eyes widened. "Is Meadow going to have puppies with Rok?"

"I'm afraid they shall appear quite normal. However, they will most likely take after their father, given the Were gene tends to be dominant even when mixed with human."

"When you say Pack, does this mean you all like to run wild in the woods and pee on trees marking your territory?"

"Only when we can be assured of privacy."

"Hence why you live in the boonies." She frowned as she picked at the coverlet. "Bruce and his gang chose to be in the city, though. And your sister... is she a wolf, too?"

He nodded. "And my mom."

"Holy shit." She seemed to be saying that a lot.

"You okay, princess?"

"Just a bit overwhelmed. I get the impression there's a ton I still don't know."

"Good thing we have a lifetime for you to learn."

"Life?" Her voice sounded faint.

"I warned you that once we slept together it would be forever."

"We didn't technically have sex."

"No, we didn't, and yet your scent is changing."

"Excuse me?"

"It's not something you'll notice. No human will. It's a Were thing. When a true mating occurs, the scent of the couple change into something that combines both of them. It's how others know to stay away."

"But we didn't have sex," she stressed. Not in person. In her head, they'd fucked a dozen times.

"We did, however, achieve mutual orgasm, and as I recall, there was cream involved." He winked.

"In other words, you marked me with jizz."

"As I recall you swallowed."

She moaned. "Don't remind me. I can't believe I let a guy who licks his balls put his tongue in my va-jay-jay."

He grinned. "I won't need to now that we've found each other."

Implying they'd be screwing. And if he was serious, screwing exclusively for life. "I don't think I'm ready for this."

"I did warn you."

"I thought you were being flirty and cute. There is no such sure thing as forever."

"There is when you find your true mate."

"Me?" she questioned.

"You."

"What if we hate each other in a week?"

"Doubtful."

"A month?"

He tugged her into his arms. "Don't be afraid, princess."

"I'm not afraid."

"Everything will work out. We're meant to be."

"How do you know?"

"Because I love you."

TWENTY-TWO

Asher blurted out "I love you," and her first impulse was to laugh. How could he say that? They'd known each other only days.

It felt like longer. And she could understand even why he'd think it might be love. The intensity between them was unlike anything she'd ever experienced.

Still...

Her rebuttal? "It's lust."

"I know what lust feels like. Trust me, this is more than that."

"Is it, though? I know nothing about you. Or you of me."

"Well, I know you have an extensive family, and I like your Aunt Cecily."

"What you don't know is my parents were

addicts. Gambling and drugs. They thought nothing of abandoning me as an inconvenience. My family took turns taking me in when I was young. As I got older, I learned to handle things on my own."

"In my case, my dad died when we were young. I started working for cash at twelve so I could help out."

"Is this a competition on rough childhoods?"

"More like letting you know I understand struggling."

"Yet I don't get the impression your mother neglected you."

"And I'll bet your extended family did their best to offer support even if you rejected it."

She scowled. "As if I didn't know they were the ones putting food in our fridge when I was at school." Her parents never thought of the basics like using money for groceries. Her grandparents were the ones to leave a new backpack filled with supplies by the foot of her bed the day before school began each fall.

They talked all that morning, emerging for food and a bit of socialization with the others before they took off. Given Astra started having Braxton Hicks the night before, Meadow and her gang—because like fuck would she think of Amarok as boss—decided to head home a day early.

Val wasn't ready, not with her head still sore, and to be honest, she needed more time to process things. No surprise, Asher stayed behind with her. Not pressuring her to do anything but talk.

"Ask me anything." He meant it, too.

She started out with soft questions, and not the ones he expected. She wanted to know the man. First kiss. First fuck. First love was the one he finally grumbled about.

"Melinda. In my defense, she never showed her shitty side."

"Don't feel bad. I dated a douchebag I thought I loved, too."

"Looking back, I don't know how I ever thought it was love." He shook his head.

"And yet you're convinced that's what you feel now."

"There's something between us, princess. It exhilarates. Terrifies. Makes me wants things I never wanted before."

Funny how he managed to articulate the same thing she felt.

While she'd had a shower that morning, she needed another after dinner because lobster had to be eaten with the hand and the butter sauce dripped all over her front. It provided an escape from Asher, not that she minded his presence. More what he did to her being around, a state of awareness that needed handling.

She left him clearing up their dinner and hit the shower. She left the door open, a subtle invitation since she wasn't ready to simply ask. She stripped and stood under the hot spray, letting it sluice down her body.

Nice but not as nice as his hands would feel. Sigh. Her state of arousal wasn't aided when she imagined Asher in the shower with her, his big body pressing against hers, his hands stroking.

Between her legs throbbed, and touching it herself only made it worse. Because she wanted him. Wanted his tongue licking and sucking.

She made do with her fingers, stroking between her nether lips as she leaned against the tile wall. She dipped in and out before stroking her clit exclusively, giving it the friction that tightened her pussy.

A slight noise opened her eyes, and despite the fogging of the glass wall, she saw Asher standing in the doorway. Watching. Eyes at half-mast. Despite being caught watching, he didn't look away.

She crooked a finger.

He stripped as he approached, revealing the lean lines of his body. He joined her in the shower, making the large space suddenly a lot more crowded.

Was she doing the right thing?

Yes, was the reply as his mouth met hers, a soft, languorous embrace that kept her back against the wall with a leg hooking around his waist. His body pressed between her thighs as he kissed her. She dug her nails into his shoulders.

He was a complex man. Maybe not the right one. Yet no denying with Asher she felt alive. Wanted. And so needy she took control, skimming her hands over his rock-hard physique. Her lips followed the path of her hands. Nipping. Sucking. Claiming that smooth flesh.

"Princess," he murmured before dropping down so that his face was level with her pubes. She might have been more disappointed if she didn't know what to expect.

He blew on her, a hot breath that drew a shiver. He pressed a kiss against her mound, and she grabbed him by the hair to hiss, "Don't tease me."

He lashed her with his tongue, lapping at her already swollen clit. His hands anchored her hips when she jerked, holding her in place that he might keep licking. He let his tongue explore her clit, slipping between nether lips to probe deeper.

But it wasn't enough. She keened and arched. He got the hint and replaced his tongue with fingers and then proceeded to suck her clit, bringing her to the edge of orgasm.

And then he stopped.

"No!"

"I'm not done." He chuckled as he rose, a wet god who cupped the back of her head and dragged her close for a kiss. His cock pressed against her lower belly. Hard and ready.

"Fuck me," she demanded.

"As my princess commands."

He lifted her leg once more to sit around his waist. He had to dip a little to get the right angle with his cock. He found the spot and slid in, thick and long, filling her, stretching her, going deep enough she clawed at him. He had no problem finding and hitting her sweet spot. Grinding deep. Swirling it against her G. Making her gasp and shudder as he brought her back to the edge. Held her there.

Held her on the edge of pleasure while she clung to him.

"Give it to me," she panted.

His fingers dug into her ass as he ground harder. Faster.

Her breath came in hot pants. Then she wasn't breathing at all. She came so hard she couldn't move. When she did finally exhale, he caught the sound with his mouth and his hips pistoned one last time, thrusting so deep he triggered a second explosion.

A boneless creature, she might have gotten sucked down the drain if he didn't hold her up.

"You okay?" he asked softly.

"Mmm." About all she could manage.

He chuckled. "Let's go to bed."

That sounded like an excellent plan, especially since it meant she could push him onto his back and truly explore his body. Then ride him until they both yelled.

Eventually, they collapsed. Sated for the moment. Happy. Together.

Could it be like this forever?

The next morning, before she'd come to a decision, someone bellowed her name.

TWENTY-THREE

This time it wasn't Meadow and gang waiting in the living room.

Aunt Cecily, of the impressive lungs, stood by a table laden with breakfast items. Yet she wasn't why Val's stomach clenched. Grandma and Grandpa sat on the couch, stern and dressed in their Sunday best rather than at home preparing to go to church.

Why had they come?

"I am assuming you have a good reason for barging in?" Val asked.

Aunt Cecily glanced past Val to the doorway at her back and tilted her head.

Oh. This was about Asher.

Her lover.

The werewolf.

Who gave her the most incredible sex.

And claimed they shared some epic bond.

A problem who still lived in the boonies and expected her to spend forever with him.

Val liked Asher. Might even be happy at that ranch for a while. But not forever. Val knew herself. It wouldn't be long before boredom set in. She wasn't the happy-homemaker type and fuck farming. Grocery stores existed for people like her. As for her other home economic skills, cooking in her case equaled burning. When it came to cleaning, she hired someone to do hers.

What about her career? Val thrived handling the office of the law firm owned by her uncle. An office manager for a divorce lawyer did more than just order stationary and ensure the phone bill got paid. In her case, she also pulled case files, sat in on some meetings to ensure a feminine perspective, even sometimes did undercover work when the case involved a possible cheating husband or wife. Val was everyone's type.

Could she give that up for Asher? For love?

Asher must be mistaken. He was in lust. So was she. Soul mates and forever... She didn't believe in that. Then again, a day ago she didn't believe in werewolves either.

"Good morning. What brings you here?" she

asked, heading for the buffet. Hopefully there was coffee strong enough to survive the next hour.

"Who is this man you're engaged to?" Grandma didn't mess around.

Val took her time answering, grabbing a buttered piece of toast from under a dome. A little moist due to the steam caused by the heat of the slices. She bit a piece off and chewed as she poured a coffee, knowing her delayed answer drove her grandparents crazy.

But it would also make her grandpa proud. After all, he was the one to teach her the art of dangling people. It made her wonder what the old man would think of Asher. She had a feeling they'd like each other quite a bit.

"I see Aunt Cecily just couldn't keep her mouth shut." She shot a glare at her favorite relative aside from her grandparents.

Cecily grinned and shrugged, not one bit repentant.

"Maybe if you didn't keep secrets, she wouldn't spill them by accident," Grandma snottily replied.

That caused Val to snort. "You're just peeved I didn't tell you before anyone else."

"Your grandfather and I practically raised you." Yup, Grandma was miffed.

"You did." They kept trying even as her parents kept failing. It made Val strong. Strong enough to not ever give in to things she didn't want. Such as living in the woods.

"Who is he?" Grandma didn't bother to hide her ire.

Before Val could reply, Asher emerged, fully clothed and smiling. "Good morning. You must be the famous grandparents I've heard about. Such a pleasure to meet you and thank you so much for taking such good care of Val as a child. She's a remarkable woman because of your efforts."

He disarmed her grandparents with frightening ease. Not only managing to impress Grandpa with his wit and confidence but charming Grandma to the point she patted his hand and even smiled.

Inevitably, things turned awkward, as the old lady just had to say, "I keep hearing the word engaged, but where is the ring?"

Val almost groaned. She opened her mouth, ready to admit they didn't have one, when Asher reached into his pocket and pulled out a box.

"Given our whirlwind courtship, I had to wait until she was busy with Meadow to go shopping for one. But first..." He faced her grandfather. "Sir, I realize you've yet to really get to know me, however, feel free to look into me as much as you'd like. You'll find me hardworking and loyal."

It was Aunt Cecily who said, "According to his

friends, he sends almost his entire paycheck to his mom to help her out."

"Leaving nothing for his wife." Grandma gave him a hard stare.

"I would never have Valencia want for anything," Asher defended.

"And I don't need a man's money," she grumbled.

"Nor does she need my permission." Grandpa snorted. "So don't ask me. I'm not the one who gets to decide."

Which led to Asher turning to Val, the most disarming smile on his face.

Oh no.

He wasn't.

He did.

Dropped to a knee and looked up at her. "I'm glad your closest family is here right now."

"Meadow's not."

"But Meadow already knows about this. Who do you think helped me choose the ring?"

He opened the box to show a sapphire set in a delicate white gold band. An almost perfect match for the dream ring from her wedding album.

"How?" she whispered. "You were never alone with Meadow."

"She has a phone. I hit a few stores and told them of her description. Then I texted her pictures until she told me I'd found the right one. She also knew your ring finger size."

He plucked it free and held it aloft.

Her heart thumped.

For some reason, this was making it too real. He was going to ask. What would she say?

"Valencia, from the moment I met you, I knew you were the one for me."

"I yelled at you for like twenty minutes that first time."

He grinned. "Do you know how rare it is for a woman to do that?"

"You are way too pretty for your own good."

"Agreed. And you are much too sexy. Which is why we're perfect for each other. Marry me, princess. Let me be your forever Wookie."

She panted. Hyperventilating in panic for the first time in her life. Commitment. Giving up everything she knew. All she'd worked for.

For the right man.

He held out the ring, and she extended her hand. It slid on, a perfect fit. Her grandmother sniffled. Aunt Cecily whistled. Grandpa, well, he stood and cleared his throat.

"I expect we'll get a wedding invitation shortly." He helped Grandma up.

Val blinked at them. "That's it? He proposes, I say yes, and you leave?"

It was grandma who offered a knowing grin as she said, "You forget, we were young once. I remember what happened after your grandfather asked me."

Gag.

TWENTY-FOUR

ASHER THOUGHT FOR SURE VAL WOULD DIE OF embarrassment as she complained. "Argh. My eyes. My innocence."

"Don't be such a prude," her grandmother said quite primly.

Cecily outrighted laughed then choked as Grandma said, "After Antonio asked me is when Cecily was conceived."

"TMI. TMI," Val yelled as she stomped into the bedroom.

Asher, left behind, shrugged. "She's over-whelmed."

"She's very precious to us." The genial conversa-tion turned dark as Grandpa lowered his voice to say, "Hurt her and they won't find your body."

"I would die before I ever harmed her."

"Good. You'll ensure she visits us regularly," her grandfather stated, not asked.

"Of course."

"Tell him they have to use the hotel for the wedding," Cecily loudly whispered.

"He'd be an idiot to not take advantage of the family discount," Grandmother declared.

It took a few more minutes before he could escape and see where Val had gone. He found her squashing clothes into her suitcase.

"Your grandparents want to say goodbye before they leave."

"Did they properly threaten you?"

"I'm a dead man if I don't make you happy."

Her lips finally twitched in amusement. "Guess you'd better get to work."

"As my princess commands." He winked.

They said goodbye to her family, and as they shut the door, she sighed and said, "Glad that's over."

"Me, too, because now we can celebrate."

"Like hell we are."

"Are you still traumatized by what your grandma said? Even old people were young once."

"Not that!" she exclaimed, advancing on him. "You. This." She stared at her hand and the ring glinting her finger.

"Looks good."

"It's gorgeous, but it's what it symbolizes I'm not sure I like. It's another way of claiming me." She wrinkled her nose. "I don't want to be owned."

"As if I'd dare even try. Think of it more like we belong to each other."

"I'm still not sure I'm ready, though," she said softly.

For a woman used to being in control, the speed with which her life changed had to be scary. He took her into his arms. "I know it's terrifying. I'm scared, too. But we'll handle it. Together. Or I'll be dead, and you can move on."

Her laughter came with a kiss. But he could sense the underlying tension.

They made love. Twice. And for a while, the anxiety in her eased. However, it returned the closer they got to the ranch. He felt it through their bond even as he struggled to pinpoint the cause. It led to him asking, "What's the plan for after the wedding?"

"Wedding? But we haven't even talked about a date," she squeaked, jerking the wheel, almost putting them in a shallow ditch. The tires caught and spun gravel before they found the road again.

"Not our wedding. Meadow's." Although her reaction let him know she still struggled with the idea of them being together. Over time, she'd come to accept it. Hopefully.

"I hadn't really thought about it. At some point, I'll have to go back to my place and deal with my work and stuff. I have a lot of furniture and personal effects that won't fit in the cabin. I guess they could go in storage." Her lips turned down, and he began to grasp the issue.

"We don't have to live on the ranch. We could get a house in town."

Her lips twisted before she caught herself and said too brightly, "Are you sure? That's a helluva commute for work."

No shit. And probably not the time to tell her the idea of going back to mucking in fields after a few high-adrenaline days in the city didn't appeal, especially since he could tell she still hadn't come around to the idea of living on the ranch as part of the pack.

Perhaps Kit's demand he oversee the Festivus Pack wasn't a bad one. At least for a little while as he and Val got used to each other. It might be less of a shock to her to have the amenities she was used to.

Before he could broach it, she pulled over and slid her hand up his thigh to his crotch. "Want to test how big the back is?" Plenty big once they shoved aside the luggage.

After the sex, he didn't want to ruin her mood with talk of where they'd live. Plenty of time to figure things out before the wedding. They drove the rest of the way listening to rock songs that she knew a surprising amount of lyrics to. So did he, and they made a great duet. Pity there were no karaoke bars anywhere within a hundred-mile radius.

The reminder of distance made him think of his sister, mother, and the new niece he'd left behind. He missed them already. Hated he wouldn't be close by to see the little girl grow. But at least now he could visit. It was just a matter of making the crazy-long drive.

They pulled in front of the ranch house in silence.

He glanced at her. "You ready?"

She stared out the front and took a deep breath before saying, "Yeah."

He should have talked to her then. Should have known something wasn't right.

Because, by morning, she and her SUV were gone. The note said, *I'm sorry. I can't do it. Not even for you. Val*

TWENTY-FIVE

Val cried most of the drive home. Big snotty tears that she hated.

A part of her wanted to turn around and go back. Asher would be crushed. Hell, she was fucking wrecked.

However, she knew if she returned to that ranch, it wouldn't be long before she snapped. Not because the place wasn't beautiful. It totally was. And as a vacation spot, she could have handled a few weeks, maybe even a month. But knowing it was forever?

She fled.

Fled like a coward in the night rather than look Asher in the eye and tell him the truth. Because he was her weakness. If he asked, she'd stay and make them both miserable, killing whatever sparked between them.

You mean like I killed it by leaving him abruptly? Too late now.

Her house, impeccable as always, tended inside and out, waited for her at the end of the cul-de-sac. Behind her, past her rear fence, was Crown Land. Forest mostly, giving her privacy.

The garage opened with the push of a button, and she drove right in. The door closed as she leaned her head on the steering wheel, out of tears, yet still grieving the breakup.

Asher would have woken hours ago at this point. Read the note. Known she'd left.

She glanced at her phone. He'd not called. Neither had Meadow, who also got a tiny note that said, *Something came up. Will be back in time for the wedding.*

No one contacted her at all because she didn't belong in their world. Their Pack.

Story of her life. Val had always been on the outside looking in. Aloof because caring led to disappointment and abandonment. Like the time things got good with her mom for once. She'd come out of rehab and promised things would be better. It lasted six months. Then she left without a word.

In time, Asher would have seen she wasn't special. Just like her parents, he would have decided she wasn't worth it and left her, too. Then what? She'd have been alone in the boonies with nothing. Better she be where she had a job and a home.

Alone.

Good thing she knew a cure to loneliness. She'd just cracked the bottle of wine when someone knocked.

She eyed the door. Probably a salesperson. She poured a glass.

"I know you're in there, princess."

Asher?

Excitement filled her. Fear, too. Only a couple of reasons he'd have followed. To ask for the ring back or yell at her, probably both.

Don't be a coward. She clenched her fist as she flung open the door.

He stood on her stoop, dressed in a leather coat, goggles on top of his head, his jeans molding his thighs.

"What are you doing here?" Looking deliciously sexy. It was all she could do not to drag him inside.

"What do you think I'm doing here, princess?"

Her lips turned down. "You want the ring back."

"No, you idiot. I'm here because you are." He rolled his eyes.

"How did you get here so quick?"

He stepped aside to show off the crotch rocket

parked in her driveway. "I might have been going a little fast to make sure I caught up."

"You shouldn't have bothered." She strode away from him, going for her wine. "I'm not going back. That is, I will for the wedding, but that's it. I'm sorry, Asher. I care for you. Like a crazy amount. However, I'll die if I have to live hidden away in the forest."

"I agree. Which is why I'm moving out."

She whirled and blinked. "Moving where?"

"Here." His slow grin warmed her head to toe. "Make room in your closet, princess, because you're going to have to share."

Was he implying what she thought? "But your job—the Pack—"

"Will do just fine without me. It's not like I'm dead. I'm just moving on to other things with my mate. You are more important."

"You'd give up your life for me?" Her voice emerged in the smallest of whispers.

"Yup."

Her lips turned down. "I must seem like such a bitch for not doing the same."

His arms tugged her close. "What you are is a strong, independent woman with a career and family of her own. And I'm just the adaptable kind of guy who thinks that's awesome and wants to support it."

"Really?" Hope fluttered.

"Fuck yeah. And before you think I'm going to be a mooch, I've already got a job."

"What? How?"

"Let's just say there's a new sheriff in town."

"Ooh, a man of the law."

"Pack laws," he corrected with a teasing nip of her lip.

"Meaning what?" she asked, turning serious for a moment.

"Meaning, the Lykosium Council has offered me a job. Apparently, they were quite disturbed by recent events. At first, they only wanted to make me the conservator for the Festivus Pack. That job has since expanded. They now want me to be their emissary for Western Canada. I'm to ensure the Packs in Alberta and surrounding provinces behave."

"Sounds like you'll have to travel."

"Not too often. Maybe once a month for a few days. Course, it would be better if I didn't have to go alone." He eyed her with expectation.

He wanted her by his side. He was willing to move so she didn't have to. The least she could do was meet him partway. "I've always liked a bit of adventure. My cousin Lenny can give us deals on flights and car rentals."

"But can Lenny do this?" He kissed her soundly. Breathlessly.

And then did even more with his mouth and hands. Her bed ended up halfway across the room by the time they were done, but she was smiling as she snuggled Asher and said, "I love you."

Rather than pull a classic *Star Wars* and say, "I know," he uttered a fitting Wookie howl.

EPILOGUE

THE WEDDING WENT OFF WITHOUT A HITCH.

Meadow, radiant in her white gown with its lace-embroidered empire waist—which Asher knew nothing about until Val explained it in detail—appeared as if she'd burst with happiness. Rok looked uncomfortable in his suit and kept fidgeting until the music started and Meadow began her walk to him on her dad's arm.

Mr. and Mrs. Fields arrived two days before in an RV that had a few of the Pack members talking about getting some, as they were simpler to manage than adding more buildings.

Asher's place was empty, given he'd packed all his stuff and had what he needed already packed in Val's SUV. While he made the leap from ranch to city on a whim to please Val, to his surprise he fit in well with the city life and was especially fond of his new role as Lykosium Enforcer. He even had a badge that got the local Pack ladies simpering in his direction. Let them. He had eyes for only one woman.

Val stood across from him as maid of honor, misty eyed as she watched her best friend getting married. As for him and Val, they'd opted to do it in the spring because Val wanted to be wed outside when the tulips bloomed.

At the reception, he slow danced with his fiancée, his mate, his future. Hard to believe the first time they'd met he'd been scared, and yet the taming of this beta was the best thing to ever happen to him. Because love was everything.

A FEW DAYS LATER, mere paces from the main house...

Poppy walked into the cabin she shared with her brother, carrying a tin of freshly baked cookies, which she almost dropped as she realized she wasn't alone.

She fought to not tremble as she squeaked, "What are you doing here?"

A man sat in her brother's favorite chair, his hair a bright red in contrast to his cold gaze. "We meet again."

"Hardly again since we didn't speak the last time." But she remembered seeing him in that warehouse where Asher rescued Val.

Kit. No last name. A Lykosium enforcer. Here in her house. Her voice held only the slightest quaver as she asked, "What do you want?"

"Your help."

"With?"

His lips held a sly curve, and her stomach dropped as he purred, "Take a guess why the Lykosium might require your services specifically."

"No." She shook her head and hugged herself, suddenly cold. "I won't go back."

"Figured you might say that. Problem is you don't have a choice. Your aid is required."

Tears welled as she whispered, "I'd rather die."

"As well as condemn others, apparently."

"I can't help you." She did her best to stem the tremors that chilled as he reminded her of why she'd fled to what some considered the edge of the world.

"I'll give you time to think about it." Kit stood suddenly, too tall and imposing. Not a friend like Amarok and the others.

"I don't need time to know the past should remain buried." Because, like bodies, it only stank more with age.

He stared at her long enough that she shivered. With fear, but also awareness. The scent of him. The breadth. The strength.

"I'll be back." And with that ominous statement, he left. It was only then she noticed that he left behind a faint whiff of fox.

And a certainty that had her swallowing hard.

I think he might be my mate.

It's time to find out more about the mysterious Kit and our wounded flower, Poppy. I wonder what kind of wild romantic adventure we can expect in *Enforcer Unleashed*.

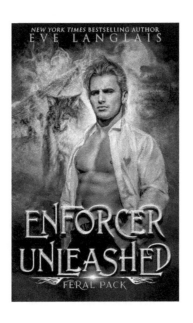

FOR MORE INFO on this book or more Eve Langlais titles, please visit,
EveLanglais.com.

CPSIA information can be obtained
at www.ICGtesting.com
Printed in the USA
LVHW080742200223
739907LV00035B/791